The Rose Garden

The Rose Garden

Linda Boulter

Matador
Unit E2 Airfield Business Park,
Harrison Road, Market Harborough,
Leicestershire. LE16 7UL
Tel: 0116 279 2299
Email: books@troubador.co.uk
Web: www.troubador.co.uk/matador
Twitter: @matadorbooks

ISBN 978 1803135 564

British Library Cataloguing in Publication Data.
A catalogue record for this book is available from the British Library.

Printed and bound in Great Britain by 4edge Limited
Typeset in 11pt Adobe Jenson Pro by Troubador Publishing Ltd, Leicester, UK

Matador is an imprint of Troubador Publishing Ltd

Dedicated to Bill, Kim and Chloe and
to great friends and relatives near and far.

Contents

—∿—

There's no stopping me now!

—∿—

I WROTE A book of twenty short stories during the lockdowns of 2020/21 whilst recovering from a cancer operation and treatments. "The Red Rose" was sold for a children's charity the Joseph Cooper Trust. For a first attempt, I was extremely happy with its sales, donations to the charity and kind words I received.

So, this is my second attempt. The title "The Rose Garden" came from many family holidays in Portugal where my daughters would give me a glass of rosé wine on their hotel balcony and play the song *Rose Garden* through their speakers (one of my all time favourites).

Happy days, Happy memories!

All of these stories are fiction although some are written with friends old, new and sadly departed, in mind. There are a couple of tributes to friends who have meant alot to me. Hopefully, there is some humour with the stories of the day centre antics and Josephine Blunderbus, the crazy chauffeur!

My years of working in health and social care as an

Occupational Therapist has inspired some of the stories particularly Hidden Disabilities.

When I wrote 'The Red Rose' some lovely friends read and proofread the manuscript and I was getting paranoid about every comma being in place! This time some of my friends have read a selection of the stories and gave me advice and helpful hints. This book, though, I have decided that if it is not word and comma perfect, it doesn't matter. It is my work and my style and it is written to raise funds for a very worthy local charity.

The proceeds, every penny from the sales will be donated to Age UK Leicester Shire and Rutland.

I hope you enjoy the book!

Me, with daughters Kim and Chloe!

A message from Tony Donovan - CEO Age UK, Leicester Shire & Rutland

—⚬—

A VERY SINCERE thank you to Linda for kindly donating the proceeds of her book to Age UK Leicester Shire & Rutland.

2022 sees the charity celebrate its 70th Anniversary. Set up to enhance quality of life whilst supporting vulnerable older people to continue living at home. Services provided by Age UK Leicester Shire & Rutland are many and varied. They include drop-in centres, information and advice support, lunch clubs, respite care, home care (help with cleaning, shopping and personal care) foot care, day care, dementia support services, advocacy and carer support.

During these very challenging times for voluntary sector organisations, Age UK Leicester Shire & Rutland has become increasingly reliant on its charity shops and donations from the public to fund the services provided. For many they are a lifeline. Without them, many people would be unable to cope and sadly have to go into care.

On behalf of the charity a very big thank to Linda and to all of you for supporting our efforts.

Tony Donovan

The Rose Garden

—⚬—

"SHALL I START cutting up these banana cakes, Chris?" Rose asked.

"Yes, you might as well get a plate of cakes ready, you can put some cling film over, then we will be ready for when people want them."

Chris replied whilst putting cups and saucers out on the work surface.

It was eight o'clock one Thursday morning and Chris was opening her house up to friends, family and passers by to raise money for a local charity. This was her second year of 'open house'. It had been so successful the previous year, raising thousands of pounds, she decided to do it again, despite it being extremely hard work. Chris had many friends and they all mucked in and did their fair share to help her make it a great day.

This year Chris felt more supported by the chosen charity because their assistant fundraising manager was coming along and staying for an hour or two to chat with the supporters. It was also a beautiful, warm day, late June in the year 2008.

Some of Chris's other friends arrived and they all got stuck in with their allocated jobs. They had all been at the house the previous day preparing for the big day. The large dining table was covered with bric a brac. There were handmade knitted garments hanging up and on rails. In the lounge there was a big raffle and a higher/lower game which Chris's husband had made. There was more bric a brac on tables in the hallway and utility room, with the kitchen all set out to serve refreshments. Rose had her apron on, was in good spirits and nearly ready to serve drinks and cakes. Chris went into the lounge to take her other helpers a hot drink, Rose opened the back door and took her mug of coffee outside for a few minutes of quiet time on her own. She was so grateful for Chris's friendship, particularly since she had lost her beloved husband Gerald who had passed away the previous year. She clutched her mug tightly and felt tearful. She looked around the back garden to try and take her mind off crying, she didn't want anyone to see her with red eyes. The back garden was mainly paved with a little grassy area but there was a small bed with a beautiful rose bush in it. Looking at the roses made her almost well up again. Gerald used to buy her a bunch of roses at least once a month just because she was called Rose. No matter how hard she tried to look after them, they soon drooped over and looked awful in their pretty vase. She used to wish he would buy her chrysanthemums because they always lasted no matter where you displayed them. She smiled to herself at the thought of drooping roses!

"Are you alright Rose?" Chris was walking towards her. "I wondered where you had gone."

"Yes I am Chris and thank you."

"Thank me for what, Rose?"

"For being a good friend."

Chris linked her arm through Rose's and the both headed back to the kitchen.

"Your rose bush is gorgeous Chris, the flowers are such a lovely colour."

"That's funny you should say that because as you know, gardening is not our thing, which is why most of the garden is paved but that rose was given to me by a friend Rachael, for my birthday a few years ago, she's an occupational therapist, and that rose represents their profession. It's got a name but I can't remember at the mo. I don't see her very often because she's always working, but she will be here later so you can ask her."

Chris then dashed off to welcome some people who had just walked in through the open front door. After that, the day got into full swing, many people arrived and Rose never stopped working in the kitchen.

Around mid morning the assistant charity fundraising manager arrived. He talked to one or two of the helpers and mooched around, then went outside and chatted to a couple of Chris's friends who had turned up to support her and were sitting outside in the back garden with their drinks. He grabbed a chair and spoke with them for about half an hour, then briefly waved goodbye to Chris, who was busy selling raffle tickets and left. Chris was a bit miffed that he hadn't made much of an effort to mingle and had spent most of his time outside. She felt that in his position he should have made an effort to chat to many of the supporters particularly as the house was pretty full of people when he arrived. Chris needed to forget her anger as she tore off another five strips of raffle tickets.

"Do you want pink or blue tickets?" she asked another one of her friends who had just arrived. "Or a mixture of both?"

Just after lunch, it went a bit quieter and there were just a couple of visitors who had made their purchases and were sitting on the settee, with drinks, chatting to the helpers. It gave Rose a chance to cut up more cake and get the kitchen tidied up a bit. Once she had finished, she looked out of the kitchen window and her eyes diverted to the roses. It was so beautiful, clusters of candy floss pink. Suddenly, she was brought out of her daydreaming.

"Hi, do you think I could have a coffee and a piece of that lovely chocolate cake please?"

"Oh, I'm sorry, I was just admiring the roses, they are so beautiful. Of course you can, I'll just boil the kettle." Rose replied to the lady standing in the kitchen doorway.

"I'm glad you like them, I gave it to Chris as a present on one of her birthdays. It is called the Elizabeth Casson rose, it represents my profession and was named after one of its founders. I'm Rachael by the way"

"Nice to meet you Rachael. Yes, Chris told me you gave the rose bush to her, but she couldn't remember the name of it"

Rachael walked towards the window and looked for herself.

"Yes, you are right, it was only a small plant when I gave it to Chris, it's definitely done really well, looks lovely."

The two women chatted whilst Rachael enjoyed the homemade chocolate cake, washed down by the coffee. Rose talked to Rachael about her late husband Gerald buying her roses because they were her namesake, but they never lasted long in the vase, always drooping or just turning brown.

The afternoon finished off with a steady stream of visitors. Chris's husband arrived home after work with a big bag of fish and chips for the helpers. The helpers had a break whilst they enjoyed the food. Visitors mingled and chatted, giving the helpers some time to finish their meals. Soon, they were back to taking the money and eventually when it got to eight o'clock

Chris went to draw the raffle. Some of the winners were still there. Chris's husband put the prizes of the absent people in a box and they would deliver them over the next few days.

Eventually, with the last of the visitor's all gone, the helpers started to clear up what they could. Chris and a couple of helpers were going to finish clearing up the following day.

The helpers finally went home, after a very long but successful day.

Rose was last to go. Chris and her husband were aware that Rose was very lonely since Gerald had passed away. They didn't have any children, although Chris always got the impression that it wasn't by choice. They were a very devoted couple and Gerald had been very active in the community and spent some of his free time driving elderly people to the local hospital for their appointments. Chris was aware that Rose had regrets about her and Gerald not buying their own house. They lived in a housing association flat quite near to Chris. The flat was beautiful inside, but in later years Rose had mentioned to Chris that she wished they owned it or had bought a small house somewhere else. On one occasion when Rose visited Chris, not long after Gerald had passed away, she confided in her that she would have loved to have a little shrine she could visit to sit quietly with her thoughts next to Gerald. She said that his remains were laid to rest in a crowded crematorium and she didn't feel she could sit with him and their memories.

Chris was exhausted, and at ten o'clock she and her husband just left the downstairs as it was and went off to bed. When Chris flopped wearily into bed, she couldn't get to sleep. Her mind was going over the events of the day and she wondered how much money they would finally end up with, after a count up and also rounding up the donations she had been promised from people unable to attend. Her mind then went to the assistant fundraising manager and she still felt a bit annoyed with his lack of enthusiasm for her event. He could have mingled more, not just take his drink outside, ignoring the supporters inside. She thought that the days of charities working with the 'grassroots' fundraisers were coming to an end. Some of the charities, as they grew in size, seemed in her eyes to be more interested in obtaining large sums of money from businesses and grants rather than associating themselves with what she called, 'the small people'. She wondered whether he had wanted to come at all because a small event wouldn't raise enough money to make it worth his while. Or maybe she was just tired and would think differently tomorrow.

The next morning, Chris woke up and found her husband had already got up and left for work. She looked at the bedside clock and was shocked to see it was just after nine o'clock. She leapt from the bed and quickly dressed. Her two friends were coming round at ten o'clock to help her clear up. After a quick wash she went downstairs and ate a hurried breakfast. Her friends turned up on time and they spent the following few hours putting the house back to normal. When her husband came home at five o'clock, he suggested that they go to a pub that night for a meal, it was a beautiful summer's evening. They sat in a comfortable corner of the pub after ordering their food. When they had finished the meal, they sat chatting about how the previous day had gone, then they both looked up and saw Rachael was walking towards them. She had come into the lounge area to buy some drinks because the bar was very busy.

"Hi guys, didn't expect to see you both here tonight! We come for the music which starts shortly in the bar. Come and join us."

Chris looked at her husband and smiled. She just wanted to go home, but didn't want to offend Rachael so they both got up, picked up their glasses and followed Rachael through to the bar where Rachael's husband was sitting. The band played for about twenty minutes before the interval. The final song before the break was "Rose Garden." It was a big hit in the sixties. After everyone had finished applauding Rachael turned to Chris.

"It just reminded me of your friend Rose, Chris. She told me the story of her husband buying her roses because it was her name."

"Yes, she certainly loved the rose bush you bought me for my birthday a few years ago. She would like a little area to sit and think of Gerald because she lives in a flat with no garden."

The four of them continued to chat before the music started up again.

"Are you still working in the community Rachael?" Chris asked.

No, I have been working in the hospital for the past six months, rehab. I just wanted a change."

"Rose's husband used to drive there most days," Chris said to Rachael. "He was a volunteer driver and used to take elderly patients for their appointments. Bless him, Gerald was a lovely man."

The music started up again and eventually, much to Chris's relief, it came to an end. The four of them walked together from the pub towards the car park. Just before they said their goodbyes Rachael turned to Chris.

"I've had an idea. The hospital has large grounds, why don't I ask if we could plant some roses in the grounds and make a memorial for Gerald there? Especially as he was there on a regular basis helping people. It's only two miles away and on the bus route, Rose could go when she wanted."

"What a wonderful idea, Rachael. Let me know how you get on," Chris replied. "See you soon."

About a week later, Rachael rang Chris and explained that she was disappointed to be turned down by the hierarchy at the hospital about the planting of roses. Chris thanked Rachael for trying and said she would see her soon.

Chris continued to see Rose on a regular basis and noticed she was getting really down about living in the flat on her own. She missed Gerald and their life they had shared together. Gerald used to drive her out to garden centres and places of interest. All Chris could do was be a good friend to her and her door was always open.

One day, the assistant fundraising manager from the charity rang her to see how she was. She had already received a thank you letter for the substantial sum of money they had raised on the open house day. Chris sighed to herself when he identified himself on the phone, she hadn't really got much time for him after his lack of enthusiasm when he visited. After a few minutes of conversation, he asked if there was anything he could help Chris with in the future.

"Well actually there is. Your charity is linked to the hospital so I want to ask you to do something."

She then relayed the story about Rose and Gerald to him. How her friend Rachael, an occupational therapist at the hospital had an idea of a memorial rose bush being planted in the hospital grounds for Gerald. How it was turned down by the hospital despite the fact that Gerald gave up his spare time to volunteer, bringing patients to the hospital."

"Is that Rachael Turner, Chris? Works in rehab?"

"Yes, take it you know her?"

"Yes our paths cross sometimes," he replied. "Will see what I can do."

Chris put the handset back on its stand and smiled. 'Not a lot from what I have seen of him,' she thought.

The months passed by, Christmas came and went and by the following Spring, Chris and her helpers were planning the next open house event for the summer. They were considering supporting another charity and in discussions about which other local one to choose. She hadn't heard from the assistant fundraising manager since their phone conversation last year. They decided they would all write some ideas down and in the following weeks would make a decision between them.

One afternoon some weeks later, they all sat in Chris's lounge busy making items for the open house afternoon when out of the blue, the assistant fundraising manager rang.

"Hi Chris, Sorry I haven't been in touch, it's just been so manic."

Chris raised her eyebrows and thought 'mmm, no time for a quick call then!'

"Anyway, hope you and your helpers are all well? I would just like to invite you to a thank you lunch at our offices. You will get an official invite through the post but I just wanted to let you know the date. There are some other supporters from around the county who are also invited so we just need some numbers for catering…" They carried on the conversation and as he had rang when they were all together, Chris was able to give him the exact numbers.

Chris relayed her day to her husband over their evening meal including the invite for lunch. He suggested they all get a bus there, because none of them drove and told Chris where the bus would drop them off. The charity office was situated next to a sports ground, the other side of the hospital. Despite the group planning to choose another charity to support, they decided to put that discussion on hold until they had been for the lunch.

The day came and they all met at the arranged bus stop. When they arrived at the charity headquarters, they were led to a room where a beautiful buffet was laid out. They each took a glass of orange juice and found a table to sit at. There were 'Thank You' banners up and soon the room had filled up and everyone was happily chatting. The sun was streaming through the windows and it was a lovely atmosphere. The assistant fundraising manager mingled with everyone and spent some time displaying an interest in everyone's efforts, which pleased Chris. As some people started to leave, Chris took the bus timetable from her bag to work out which bus they could catch to get home. The assistant fundraising manager asked the ladies if they would like to have a look around before they left. They all agreed and he showed them around the building. Then, they followed him out the back door, walked past the sports ground and into the back of the hospital grounds.

"What have you got out here?" Chris asked.

They followed him towards a seat. It was a beautiful area to sit, at the back of the hospital. There were lovely trees and beautiful plants in full bloom, full of colour.

"This is what I have got here." He pointed to a circle cut out in the grass where it was filled with a bed of candy floss pink roses situated very close to the seat.

"This is for you Rose, it's your rose garden for you to sit with your memories of Gerald."

Rose was lost for words, in fact they all were and as they tried to take in the wonderful display, then they noticed a gold plaque with Gerald's name on, situated amongst the roses.

"It's beautiful, absolutely beautiful. I can't believe it. Thank you so much" Rose said as she sat down on the seat and just stared at the roses and plaque, trying to take it all in.

Just then Rachael appeared, she had just popped out from the rehab unit nearby.

"This is my partner in crime!" the assistant fundraising manager laughed.

"Wow, how did you both manage it Rachael?" Chris asked.

"Don't you worry about that, we just did!" Rachael grinned. "Note we also got the Elizabeth Casson roses too, so my health colleagues will also be directed to admire these beautiful roses."

Chris was just delighted, it made her day. It also made her think about how she had felt about changing the charity to support. It looked like there would definitely be no change. She saw the assistant fundraising manager now in a completely different light, he must have worked so hard to organise all that. It had been a fabulous day all round.

As for Rose, she absolutely loved her very own 'Rose Garden.'

Remembering Chris

A Beautiful Daughter

—◊—

JANICE WAS IRONING in the kitchen. She had put the TV on earlier, a small TV situated on a worktop in the corner of the kitchen. She wasn't watching it, it was just on for company while she worked her way through the enormous pile of washing sitting in the washing basket on the floor. Something made her stop and sit down at the kitchen table and watch. A Welsh male voice choir was singing "Cwm Rhondda." She sat there mesmerised by the choir until the whole hymn finished. Her father had sung in a male voice choir when she was a young child and this had always been her favourite. She used to joke with him, "Sing Bread of Heaven, daddy!"

Janice stood up, picked up the remote control from the worktop and turned off the TV, then sat back down on the chair at the kitchen table and put her head in her hands. She hadn't seen her father since she was ten years old. Clive, had an affair with a lady he met as the choir sang at various venues around the area. Janice's mother found out and booted him out and she never saw him again. His name was never mentioned. Janice often felt lonely in her life during her teenage years because her mother worked long hours to pay the bills. There were just the two of them. Her mother did not have any further relationships apart from in her later years, she befriended a gentleman across the road from where she lived and they used to go to garden centres for coffee several afternoons a week. Janice was so pleased because Ray was such a lovely man and they were good company for each other.

What was also sad about her father leaving, was that her mother cut off ties with her father's parents and his younger sister who had all lived in the next village. Thankfully, she had such happy memories of her mother's parents who had lived close by. She smiled to herself as she thought of them. They were such a kind, friendly folk, 'salt of the earth'. How she missed them. They certainly helped to take away the pain caused by her father's absence. They never mentioned her father's name once he had gone. It was as if every bit of her father's presence from the age of ten had just vanished.

Janice had fond memories of her father. He had been a fun dad and spent a lot of time with her, always larking around. His job meant that he did go to work abroad at times, sometimes away for as long as a week but he always made up for lost time when he came back and spoiled her when he could. He would take her for walks and they would stop at a pub. She waited on a bench outside whilst he would pop inside and come out with a bottle of coke with a straw sticking out the top for her, a beer for himself and two packets of crisps. They would sit on the bench laughing and chatting whilst they ate and drank.

Janice remembered her childhood holidays with both parents. They spent time in static caravans at various sites around the country. She smiled as she recalled one time when her father came home from his business trip and excitedly stated that one of his colleagues had offered to loan them a touring caravan for a change. "It's called a Sprite Musketeer!" he laughed. Janice recalled being around seven years old and was so excited herself when he said it was a five berth caravan and she could take her best friend if her parents agreed. Clive arranged a tow bar to be fitted on his car and eventually the touring holiday began. She and her friend, Denise, had such fun on that holiday. They toured Scotland, they walked, looked for the Lochness Monster, took a chair lift up the Cairngorms, ate loads of food and played cards in the evening. It was, in her eyes, childhood bliss. One evening they were staying at a site near a fairground where the family enjoyed the rides and they laughed all the way back to the caravan. That night whilst her mum and dad slept, she remembered her and Denise staying awake to watch the fair from their beds. Her friend was in the hammock above her. They were trying to be quiet so they didn't disturb her parents, but then her friend, trying to stifle her laughter, fell off the hammock and knocked the glass of water over, waking up her father. Even then, Clive just laughed at them and helped Denise back onto the hammock. Why did her father give all this up for another lady?

What had this lady got that made him give up his life which in her child eyes had appeared to make him happy? Why didn't he write to her or send her a birthday card? Why did he care and then not care? Why did he just disappear and not try to contact her? Maybe he started a new family with his girlfriend and had forgotten about her or just blanked out his past life? So many questions, probably never to be answered.

Janice had got married without her father to give her away. Her elderly grandfather stood in and how lovely that had been. Her own daughter, Ellie, had missed out on having Clive as a grandad. Thankfully, husband Tony's parents were fantastic grandparents to Ellie. She couldn't imagine a life without Ellie and often wondered how people can just disappear out of their children's lives.

Janice was still sitting at the table when fifteen year old Ellie walked in through the kitchen door.

"You okay mum?" she asked, looking at the washing basket and clothes hanging around and her mum just sitting at the table.

"Yes, love. I had the TV on and a hymn came on that reminded me of my dad, that's all."

Ellie fetched a glass and filled it with some tap water, then sat down opposite her mum. She sipped at the water and picked at the grapes from the fruit bowl on the kitchen table.

"Mum, why don't we try and track him down?"

"What's the point Ellie? He left when I was ten, he hasn't made any contact since and that's over thirty years ago. Yes, I suppose he could still be alive but he may have another family and not be interested in us."

"But mum, we know his name, it shouldn't be too difficult."

"Yes but if he rejects me, then how would I feel? After all, he did that when I was ten." Janice smiled at Ellie. "Let's just forget about him, Ellie, it's not worth it. Tell you what, when your dad gets home, shall we go out tonight and have a meal at the pub for a change?"

Ellie drank her water, stood up and hugged her mum.

"Yep, I'm going to get ready." She disappeared upstairs and Janice grinned when she heard the loud music coming from Ellie's bedroom. Janice made up her mind then that she was not going to mention her father to Ellie again, it was pointless. Even if he was still alive and there was every chance he could be, he had not shown any interest in her since he left so why should he now.

Several weeks later Janice was at work where she was an admin assistant in a busy social services office. A colleague called Sarah came up to her.

"Hi Janice, it's a nice day, do you fancy eating your lunch outside in a bit? We haven't had time for a catch up lately and it will be a change from dropping our crumbs on the keyboard when we continue to work whilst eating!"

"Great, Sarah, shall I see you out there around twelve thirty?"

Sarah nodded in agreement and off she went back to her computer. Janice and Sarah had always been friendly with each other since Sarah came to work at the office a couple of years earlier. She was younger than Janice but they got on well.

The office was situated at the back of a country park and there were a few bench seats on the grass for office staff to sit. Just after twelve thirty the two women sat out and ate their lunch, catching up on the latest news. The thirty minutes flew by.

"Janice, shall we go somewhere one evening and have a night out again? It's been a while and we can catch up properly?" Sarah enquired, as they stood up ready to walk back into the office.

"Yes, what a good idea Sarah. Ellie is going to Wales for a week with the school in a few weeks. How about then? It will take my mind off missing her!"

"That would be great, text me tonight Janice and let me know the week she is away and we can arrange an evening."

The two ladies then went their separate ways inside the office.

Later that evening the two of them, through text messages, arranged to meet for a meal on the Wednesday of the week that Ellie was going to be on her school trip. Janice now felt that the week Ellie was away was getting quite full, which was good because she would miss her so much. Tony was going to take her to a concert on the Thursday and Ellie would be home on the Saturday lunchtime.

The time came for Ellie to go on the trip. Tony and Janice took Ellie to her school where the bus was leaving from. Janice had given Ellie a packed lunch for the journey. They both kissed her before she boarded the bus and waved to her as the bus pulled away. Janice felt as she normally did when Ellie went on trips, just empty. Tony knew how Janice felt when Ellie went on trips, so he grabbed Janice's arm, and led her to the car.

"I'm going to take you for lunch and a coffee," Tony told her.

They went to a lovely quaint country pub and after lunch Janice felt a bit happier, telling herself Ellie loved going on the school trips and would have a great time.

Janice actually enjoyed the week, far more than what she had expected. She had a lovely evening out with Sarah, an enjoyable concert with Tony and also with working, the week had flown by.

Saturday lunchtime arrived and it was time to drive to the school and collect Ellie from the bus. Once they had returned home, they all sat at the kitchen table to eat the sandwiches Janice prepared earlier and listen to Ellie's rundown of the week away. About five minutes into the conversation Ellie put down her half eaten sandwich.

"Mum, I have something to tell you, but I'm not sure how you will take it."

"Try me then Ellie," Janice laughed and put down her sandwich, whilst Tony carried on eating looking bemused.

"Well, most evenings we spent in the hotel, it was fun, they put music on and we could dance, like a disco with flashing lights.

On the Thursday evening after tea we went on a coach to the cathedral in the city. None of us were enthusiastic because we had such fun on the previous evenings and it sounded dull to go to a cathedral and watch choirs. But anyway we sat near the back of the cathedral because there were lots of children from other schools there. There were a few different choirs and towards the end was a Welsh male voice choir and they sang the song you like, "Cwm Rhondda", so I did listen to that one because it made me think of you. At the end, the compere thanked the choir, who always rehearsed at the cathedral and he also thanked the conductor. Mum…his name was Clive Wiltshire."

It went quiet, Tony stopped eating.

Janice, do you think he could be your father?" Tony looked at Janice.

"No idea, but even if he was, he hasn't made any effort to make contact since he left, so it would be unlikely he would want any contact now. We wouldn't know how to get in touch, anyway."

"But mum, the compere said the choir rehearsed at the cathedral each week so let's just write him a letter and address it to him at the cathedral."

"Go for it Janice," Tony suggested. "Look, if we don't hear anything back, we can assume that it's either the wrong man or he wants no contact and we forget about him. Let's just give him a chance."

"I don't know," Janice replied.

"Please mum, he looked like such a friendly man from what I saw. I know that sounds daft but he had a nice smiley face."

Janice finally agreed and later after they had cleared up the lunch pots and sorted out Ellie's washing, they all devised a letter to Clive. It was short and started with an apology if they had the wrong man. The letter was posted and after that none of them mentioned Clive again…until three weeks later.

A letter arrived which Janice picked up off the mat when she returned from work just after three o'clock one Monday afternoon. She decided to wait until Ellie got home from school around four before she opened it. When Ellie returned she saw the letter on the table.

"Mum, this is the reply isn't it? It has a Wales postmark, why haven't you opened it?"

"Just wanted to wait for you, love, too nervous here on my own."

Ellie sat down on a chair and picked the letter off the kitchen table, opened it and read it. Janice sat on another chair watching Ellie's expression as she read. Ellie's face broke into a smile.

"Mum, he is your dad."

They both looked at eachother, then Ellie gave Janice the letter to read. It was quite long and it took Janice a while to sink in what was said.

My dear Janice, This is what I have been waiting for. When I left, I contacted your mother to make arrangements to see you but she never responded. I sent you Christmas and Birthday cards but from your letter I see you may not have been given them. I can't blame her, I left and it was not her fault, I just fell in love with Mary. But I had hoped that despite what she felt about me, she would let me see you. After getting no response, some ten years later, Mary and I left to live in Jordan when I got offered a post there. It was with a heavy heart that I went but I had hoped that when you reached eighteen you might look for me. When I retired, I couldn't bear to come back to England because of unhappy memories so we bought a place in Wales. I then joined the choir as their conductor. My late parents and my sister had tried to make contact with your mother but no response. Our only consolation was that your mother was a good mother to you. I sent her money each month for you until you were eighteen. There was never a day that went by that I didn't think of you but I respected your mother and did not want to cause any further upset. I am so thrilled that your daughter was at the cathedral concert. It has made me so happy that you have contacted me. I hope you feel we can meet. Your everloving dad xx

When they had both digested the contents Janice and Ellie talked about it. Janice was shocked to know how hard he had tried to keep in contact to which she had absolutely no knowledge. She didn't blame her mother, she had been a good mother to her. Obviously, she had been so upset when her husband had left her for Mary and that is how she chose to deal with it.

"Mum, he wouldn't know that grandma is no longer with us. We didn't put it in the letter. Shall we all meet up with him? He sounds lovely and from what I saw of him at the cathedral, he had a nice face."

Janice smiled at Ellie and thought that maybe they could meet him, but she wanted Tony to read the letter when he arrived home from work.

Six weeks later after many exchanged letters between Janice and Clive, Tony, Janice and Ellie set off on a Friday evening for a weekend stay at a hotel in Wales. They were due to meet up with Clive and Mary at a country hotel on Saturday afternoon for afternoon tea. Janice had mixed emotions, she felt sad for her lovely mum, she felt like a traitor, but on the other hand, Clive was her father. She had found out that Clive and Mary did not have any children together but had looked after Mary's son until he went to university at eighteen, some years before the couple left for Jordan.

On Saturday afternoon the three of them left their hotel to meet Clive and Mary. Janice felt so nervous her legs were shaking as she walked towards the door of the hotel where they were all meeting. Ellie held her mum's arm and none of them spoke as they walked into the foyer. Janice looked around and a couple sitting on a settee in the large reception area of the old hotel stood up and the gentleman walked towards them. Janice broke away from Ellie and rushed over to her father. They hugged and the tears flowed. Finally, they all embraced in a group hug.

Eventually, they all broke free and Clive took Janice's hand and led her, followed by the others to the table in the restaurant, all set for afternoon tea. The five of them chatted happily. They sat there all afternoon catching up on all the missed years and planning to see each other in the future. Clive explained that his work for the British Government had often taken him abroad and that was why he accepted an ongoing post in Amman, Jordan. They only came home to visit his family for a couple of weeks each year and he assured Janice that he would not have taken the job if he had been in contact with her.

Janice asked how his sister was after he explained when his parents had passed away.

"Oh Gaynor is fine, she got married a year after I had left and they had two daughters. Funnily enough, her name changed from Wiltshire to Manchester when she married Bob! Had to laugh!"

Janice was a bit stunned by that comment.

"Not many people have Manchester as a last name, funny because my friend at work is called Sarah Manchester," Janice said to Clive. Clive laughed.

"Gaynor's daughter is called Sarah!"

"Are you telling me that my friend at work, Sarah, is now my cousin?"

Janice was finding it hard to take everything in. She was sitting here with her father she thought she would never see again and then to find out that her friend is now her cousin… too much information to take in! She switched off from everything going on and her thoughts went to her lovely friend Sarah. Sarah lived with her partner and often talked about her parents but obviously she called them 'mum and dad' so Janice wouldn't have known her mother was called Gaynor, and even if she did she wouldn't have thought anything of it. Suddenly, Janice was brought out of her daydreaming by Ellie.

"Mum, mum!! Are you okay?"

"Yes, love, sorry it's just such a lot to take in! But it's all wonderful." She hugged Ellie and smiled. They all carried on chatting and laughing for several more hours before they left the hotel. They arranged further meetings with the first being Clive and Mary visiting Janice, Tony and Ellie. Clive and Mary would also talk to his sister and see if they can arrange a family reunion which would include Sarah and her partner. Janice was so happy, she felt complete now that she was reunited with her father. She was still taking in the fact she was related to Sarah. How many times do you hear the phrase 'it's a small world'. Well it certainly felt like that for Janice!

Several weeks later, Janice got home from work and pulled out her ironing board from the cupboard. She took the large washing basket piled high with washing and stood it on the floor and sighed. She wasn't a big fan of ironing and was aware that a lot of people didn't iron these days but she just felt better if clothes were pressed, so she picked up the remote control and put on the TV.

She sat down when she realised that on the repeat Songs of Praise programme, a male voice choir were singing "Cwm Rhondda." She looked at the screen and noticed that she had pressed the subtitles button by mistake, the word 'Jordan' came up on the screen as part of the hymn.

'Goodness me,' she thought. 'That was where dad went to work.'

Just then Ellie walked in from school and looked around the kitchen.

"Mum, what's happened now?"

Janice stood up, plugged the iron in, topped it with distilled water and began ironing.

"Nothing, love, I'm just so happy you put me in touch with dad. Anyway, I must iron, we need these clothes for the family reunion on Saturday. Isn't it exciting, I can't wait."

"Yes it is mum and I have got you a present to wear on Saturday, I'm going upstairs to get it."

Ellie ran upstairs and soon came down again.

Janice opened the small box and inside it was a locket. She opened up the heart shaped locket.

There was a tiny photo of her, Tony and Ellie on one side and Clive and Mary on the other side.

Janice hugged Ellie.

"It's beautiful, just like you Ellie."

Saturday eventually came. The three of them were so excited about meeting up again with Clive, Mary, Gaynor and the family and of course her friend Sarah! They were all gathering at a hotel nearby which Clive and Mary were staying for the weekend.

They all met up at twelve noon and there was so much chatter and fun over the next few hours where they ate in the restaurant, before moving to a quiet area of the hotel for further drinks.

Clive eventually stood up and asked if he could say a few words. Everyone went quiet and he beckoned Mary who was sitting with Janice and Ellie to join him.

"First I would like to say, this is such a happy day, I have felt so happy being reunited with Janice and her family. We have so much to catch up on. There is one other thing I would like to say… Mary and I are to be married and we would love Ellie to be a bridesmaid…"

Everyone clapped and cheered. Janice hugged Ellie whilst smiling at Sarah. Clive and her mother had never divorced, and now her beautiful mother was no longer here, Clive was free to marry Mary. Even though she shed a tear for her mother, she couldn't be happier for Clive and Mary. She wrapped her fingers over the locket around her neck and felt that all the years where she had felt so incomplete were now at an end.

The clapping and cheering stopped when Clive quietly began singing with his arm around Mary. The whole family then slowly began to join in with … "Guide me, O Thou Great Redeemer!!"

Free Spirit

—ᗡᗡ—

CATHY PUT ON the radio whilst she dusted the lounge. Her all time favourite Fleetwood Mac song "Everywhere" came on. She stopped in her tracks, sat down, put the duster and the ornament she had been dusting next to her on the settee. Tears came to Cathy's eyes when she was reminded by the song words, of the time when she nearly lost Martin.

Her mind went back to when she was a teenager and was at college. Martin was one of the group of students she used to hang around with. They had such fun in those days. Cathy smiled to herself at the thought of those carefree days. They did start a boyfriend, girlfriend relationship towards the end of their time at college but when Cathy finished her exams she just wanted to see the world, which Martin understood despite feeling upset. Cathy had been brought up by her father who spent his time either at work or in the pub. She had fended for herself for as long as she could remember so made up her mind she was going to travel. She felt she was a free spirit and compared herself to the song "Roadrunner."

Suddenly, Cathy was startled out of her daydreaming because talk of the devil, Junior Walker and the All Stars song "Roadrunner" came on the radio. 'What?' Cathy thought. 'How can you be thinking of a song and then it comes on the radio?'

Cathy sat listening to every word of that song. She thought of the time when she had no money and not much more than a toothbrush in her hand, as she travelled around various countries for many years from the age of eighteen. Martin was so upset when she left the town where they had both lived, but she had hardened herself and put him out of her mind. There was no accessible internet in those days so they did not keep in contact.

After years of travelling around the world, earning enough just to be able to eat and get about, Cathy felt the time was right to return home. Her father was getting older and although they had little contact during her years away she felt she needed to go home, at least for a while.

Cathy returned and went back to live with her father, who had neglected himself further and spent even more time in the pub. She found a job in the local supermarket which she considered just to be temporary until she got bored and then would probably take off again.

Working in the supermarket she heard that Martin was still single and had a good steady job in finance. One day as she was leaving the supermarket she actually bumped into him. They chatted and agreed to meet up although Cathy made up her mind that it was just two friends meeting up, nothing more. It had been too many years since they were younger carefree students.

Despite her intentions they did get back to becoming a couple again. Several months later Cathy got 'itchy feet' again. She just wanted to pack her backpack and go, even though she and Martin were so happy together. She knew she couldn't ask

Martin to give up his well paid job and she doubted he would even want to.

In a cowardly way, Cathy gave a week's notice at the supermarket, didn't tell Martin and just took off. She flew to Italy, just travelled around getting work in hospitality and again, difficult as it was, tried to put Martin out of her mind.

Two years later, she was working a lunchtime shift at a restaurant, when the song "Everywhere" came on the radio. There was something in the words of that song that made her stop in her tracks, just as if someone was calling her name. The manager of the restaurant shouted to Cathy.

"Affrettatevi Cathy." (Hurry up Cathy)

Cathy looked round and noticed customers that needed serving. A strange feeling came over her, she just had to get home. Luckily it was pay day that day, so as soon as she had collected her weeks wages, paid in cash, she told the owner she wasn't coming back and went to a travel agent to arrange a flight home.

Two days later Cathy was back home at her father's home. Nothing had changed with him, same old routine, work, pub and sleep. So why had listening to that song made her pack up and come home?

The next day Cathy went to the shops to get some supplies. Her dad's fridge and kitchen cupboards were almost empty, food was of little importance to him, the pub was.

Cathy was walking back home, when someone called out her name from behind. She turned around to see it was Martin's mum. Her heart sank, what on earth would she say to her, Cathy that had just disappeared out of her son's life…twice.

"Cathy, lovely to see you back," Martin's mum Sue said to her.

"Oh, hi Sue, how are you? Yes I am home. How is Martin? I'm sorry Sue, you must hate me."

"Cathy, I'm fine, but Martin isn't. He had an accident. He was driving home from work and had a car accident, which wasn't his fault. He's in hospital, in a coma. Cathy, before you say anything, we don't hate you and Martin wanted to wait for you, he was sure that when you had got the travelling out of your system, you would come back to him. We both knew the difficult upbringing you had and how your dad turned to drink when your mum went off with that younger man. The main thing is that you are back now."

Sue smiled at Cathy. Cathy realised after listening to Sue that this was the reason why she just had to get back home. It was Martin calling out to her to save him.

Cathy was suddenly brought back from her recollections of the past by another familiar song which came on the radio. She actually could not believe that these songs from the past that had such meaning to her, were being played literally one after another. The distinctive sound of Kate Bush singing "Wuthering Heights" was her and Martin's favourite golden oldie, a blast from the past which they both loved, going back to when they first met as students.

Cathy remembered how she felt when Sue told her about Martin. Underneath she had always loved Martin but was just not ready to settle down.

Sue and Cathy had found a bench to sit on after Sue had broken the news to Cathy. Sue told Cathy that Martin's accident required the air ambulance to airlift him to hospital. The crew landed the helicopter in the field of a local school and Sue would always be eternally grateful to them for saving his life.

Cathy agreed with Sue that she would visit Martin and she did every day, just watching and talking to Martin as he lay in the hospital bed asleep. One day Cathy asked the hospital staff if she could bring in her CD player. They agreed and that evening Cathy picked out her and Martin's favourite CD's from their time together.

Over the next few weeks Cathy put CD's on when she visited, quietly in the background. Martin carried on sleeping and Cathy spent days with him, just waiting for some flicker of movement. Cathy would talk to Martin about their time together, about her travels, anything to try and wake him up.

One morning with the sun streaming in through the window of the room in the hospital, Cathy set up her CD player. She inserted the CD by Kate Bush called "The Kick Inside." She settled down on the chair next to his bed and gently shut her eyes as the music played quietly in the background. The track "Wuthering Heights" came on and Cathy reminisced about the two of them at her house several years ago, silently listening to every word of this brilliant track. Cathy smiled as she listened to the word 'Cathy', her namesake in the song and how Martin used to mime, pretending to be Heathcliffe.

Suddenly, her thoughts were broken as the unbelievable happened…Martin softly uttered a word. Cathy shot up from the chair and Martin was mouthing "Cathy". Cathy pressed the red button and staff appeared, Martin just kept repeating "Cathy."

Cathy was immediately brought back to the present and had tears streaming down her face whilst she sat on the settee, remembering how she felt when Martin spoke her name. Cathy looked at her duster and the ornament next to her on the settee, she looked at the time, she had been sitting there for at least twenty minutes. In that time the radio station had played three tunes that were such a big part of her life and how strange that was. She stood up and put the ornament back, then carried on dusting the beautiful Welsh dresser in the lounge, picking up the family photo frames, dusting each one with care.

She was just so thankful how things turned out. Martin made a very slow recovery and Cathy moved into the house he had bought when she was travelling. He had bought the house with Cathy in his mind, he had always known she would come back to him and he would be there waiting. Cathy had nursed him back to good health and with her encouragement, love and support Martin was able to eventually return to work.

Cathy looked at the photo's as she dusted, one lovely school photo of their twin girls looking beautiful in their smart uniforms brought more tears to her eyes. What a morning this was turning out to be. She decided to make herself a drink, went into the kitchen then brought her steaming mug of coffee back into the lounge. As she did so, another tune came on the radio. It was "Wind Beneath My Wings." Such a beautiful song, she thought as she perched on the edge of the settee with her drink.

As she listened, imagining flying higher than an eagle, she thought of the air ambulance flying to save Martin's life. She then made a determined plan. They would organise an event to raise some money for the air ambulance services as a way of saying thank you. She planned in her head what they could do as a family to raise some money. She felt pleased with herself because her housework hadn't been productive that morning but other aspects had been and she was happy with that, housework can wait.

As she finished drinking her coffee, both hands clasped tightly around the mug, she decided they would have a fundraising event in their big garden. They had a large gazebo and they could borrow some more from their friends. Her and the girls could make a tombola, they had a good supply of unwanted presents. She could beg around the local businesses for raffle prizes and she could make cakes in advance, freeze them and serve refreshments from her kitchen on the day. No doubt Sue, who was a brilliant grandma, would be involved, she was a practical, hands on sort of person.

Just as she was feeling pleased with herself Martin popped home as he sometimes did in between visiting clients. Cathy looked at him, he was such a hero after what he had been through, the best husband and a great dad to the twins. She made him a coffee and excitedly told him of her plans.

"Martin I thought of you when *Wind Beneath my Wings* came on the radio. You are my hero and so are the Air Ambulance crew. They saved you and we are so lucky."

Martin put his arm around Cathy's shoulder and smiled at her enthusiasm.

"The girls will love it and I'm sure mum will help."

When Martin went back to work, Cathy decided to spend the time before she had to pick up the girls, planning the event. Over the next few weeks, in between working at her part time job and looking after the family, she worked hard on organising the event. She had begged raffle prizes from local businesses and collected bric-a-brac and unwanted presents from friends and family.

Their bedroom was being taken over by those items because there was nowhere else to store them. The house had three bedrooms and the girls each had their own bedrooms. The twins were excited when it got nearer. They were eight years old, a nice age where they liked to be helpful and they loved their grandma

Sue and were keen to help her on the day. Sue had roped in a couple of her friends to help run some of the stalls and she planned to help Cathy in the kitchen and sell raffle tickets. She would also keep the girls busy.

Eventually, the big day arrived. The weather was beautiful, not a cloud in the sky. Martin had assistance from a couple of his mates, putting up gazebos and setting out tables which they had borrowed. By one thirty, ready for a two o'clock start, the garden looked amazing. The table outside the kitchen door was filled with beautifully decorated cakes, the raffle prizes were neatly presented and set out perfectly on a yellow tablecloth. The bric-a-brac and books, all clean and tidy, were displayed with care. There were chairs dotted around in clusters around the garden where people could sit with their tea and cakes.

Just before two o'clock, people began trickling in and by three o'clock the garden was in full swing. Cathy worked non stop making hot drinks and serving cake. Sue and the girls were selling as many raffle tickets as they could. Sue's friends were selling the bric a brac, with the paperback books flying out. The time flew by and the money rolled in. At four o'clock Martin bellowed for some quiet and announced that he would soon be drawing the raffle tickets but before that he wanted to thank the supporters for attending and making it such a successful event. Cathy had only just emerged from the kitchen to have a quick break before collecting up the used cups and saucers.

"I want to thank everyone for coming today and supporting the fantastic Air Ambulance." Everyone clapped after Martin had spoken, then they could hear someone singing. From around the corner of the house a lady appeared carrying a beautiful bouquet of flowers, singing *Wind Beneath my Wings*. Her fabulous voice left everyone stunned to complete silence. She walked slowly as she sang and when she reached the end of the song she presented Cathy with the huge bouquet. Everyone clapped, cheered and whistled. Some even stood up from their chairs.

Martin grinned and felt somewhat emotional but managed to get his words out.

"Cathy, it's you that is my hero… and I want to thank you and my family for all you have done. You have worked non stop to make this afternoon a success, as well as looking after all of us and I'm sure when we count the money that a substantial amount will have been raised for the Air Ambulance service."

It went quiet as everyone in the garden had a tear in their eyes, then the lady singer began singing again. People began tapping their feet to the music. As the songs livened up they got up and began dancing and what was supposed to be an event that finished at four o'clock went on and on…and on…

Josephine, Crazy Chauffeur!

—◊◊—

JOSEPHINE'S DAY WAS going well so far. She loved being a chauffeur and driving her dignitary around to his events. It was such an unpredictable job. No two weeks were the same. There were days when there were no bookings in the diary, therefore, no work, or days where it was full on and it was definitely one of those days. Her morning had been spent driving her dignitary to a breakfast meeting, then lunch at the cathedral restaurant. But it was the big event that evening, with a member of the extended royal family in attendance, which was the highlight of the day.

Josephine had dropped her tiny Shih Tzu dog, Bon Jovi, with her friend Stella the previous evening, where he stayed the night and morning. Her mum, Olive, would have picked him at lunchtime, and he was to spend the rest of the day with her and Jospehines father. Bon Jovi didn't like staying on his own, so Josephine always made sure he had company. Both Stella and her parents loved him.

Josephine returned home mid afternoon after her busy morning. She took off her uniform, put jeans and a tee shirt on, then made herself a hot chocolate drink. She put an empty Tupperware tub next to her uniform as a reminder to take it with her that evening. When there was a meal at an event, Josephine would often pop to the kitchen afterwards and the chefs would fill her Tupperware tub with any leftovers. Some weeks Josephine didn't have to buy much food at all, it was one of the perks of her job.

She was relaxing on her red sofa when her phone beeped. She picked it up off the coffee table and read the message:

Josephine babe, just letting you know about your dad, he's hurt his hand doing some plumbing, I'm going to have to drop Bon Jovi back to you so I can take him to the hospital. I'm so sorry darling, but don't you worry about dad, he will live, just a few stitches required, love mum xx

Ten minutes later, she retrieved Bon Jovi from Olive's car. Her dad had a makeshift bandage around his hand. She kissed them both and wished them well for the hospital trip then carried Bon Jovi inside.

By now it was five o'clock, she would have to leave soon.

"Bon Jovi, you are going to have to come with me? You have to behave, baby, no barking at all."

She quickly gave Bon Jovi a small meal and took him for a short walk around the block. When she was sure he was emptied out, she returned home. Hurriedly, she put on her chauffeur uniform, smoothed down her cropped hair and put Bon Jovi in a suitable bag with his head popping out the top. She put her empty tupperware container in another compartment of the bag, ready to fill with leftovers later. She usually cycled to where the civic car was kept, but because she had to sneak Bon Jovi in, she had no choice but to take her old battered faithful car, Brucie. She put the bag with Bon Jovi in it on Brucie's front seat and placed the seatbelt around it.

As soon as she arrived at the garage, she looked around and when she was sure no one was about, she quickly put the bag in the footwell of the front seat. Once she had Bon Jovi settled, she did a check of the vehicle, a Jaguar XJ6. She had cleaned it after the lunch shift, but it had to look perfect so she studied it carefully. Once she was satisfied with the standard, she set off to pick up her dignitary. Thankfully, he only lived a ten minute drive away and then there was another ten minute drive to the Guildhall in the city. Hopefully, not long enough to set Bon Jovi off. The dignitaries changed each year. They all had their different personalities, sometimes they were chatty and fun, sometimes they were quiet and studious. This year's dignitary was what she could only describe as stuffy, with no sense of humour and rarely spoke to her.

When she arrived at his house, she immediately conducted herself in a professional way. She greeted the dignitary outside his house, put the civic chain around his neck, opened the back door of the car and once he was inside, made sure he was comfortable. They set off, and she noticed in the mirror that the dignitary was studying some papers, which didn't surprise her, with royalty present at the event. Not that he needed royalty to check papers, he was always reading papers, even when they drove through beautiful countryside. She thought he was probably the most 'boring' dignitary she had ever driven.

For no apparent reason, Bon Jovi barked a quiet 'woof'. Josephine panicked and made some 'woofing' noises herself. She felt her face and neck going red, she was feeling very warm. She glanced in the mirror and saw the dignitary raise an eyebrow.

"Are you alright, Josephine?"

"Yes, Sir, thank you, Sir," Josephine's voice came out at an unusually high pitch. She cleared her throat. The dignitary seemed satisfied and went back to his reading.

Thankfully, they arrived at their destination with no more noises from Bon Jovi. She parked up alongside the other civic cars and jumped out to open the door for the dignitary to exit.

"Thank you Josephine, see you inside at nine o'clock with the bouquet. Remember, you will pass it to me, then I will present it to our royal guest."

Josephine nearly fainted. 'Jeezz, oh no, no, no. oh goodness me, no, no, blast, how could I forget that?' Her mind went into overdrive.

The dignitary would have naturally assumed the bouquet was positioned carefully in the boot. Instead there was no bouquet and a dog in the front of the car.

Josephine had forgotten to order the bouquet which was supposed to have been picked up after the lunch shift. How did she forget that? She was mortified. It was seven o'clock and she had two hours to get the bouquet together…but what about Bon Jovi?

Someone made Josephine jump. It was Charlie, another chauffeur, tapping her on the shoulder.

Charlie was a good bloke and a good friend. She needed to confide in him, so she told him the whole sorry story.

"Josephine, you are barking mad!" Charlie roared.

"Less of the barking, Charlie! Help me."

Charlie agreed to look after the civic car and Bon Jovi whilst she set off on a hunt for a bouquet.

Josephine ran as fast as she could to the nearest Tesco Extra, she dashed in but to her dismay all the flower buckets were empty. She then remembered there was a small Sainsburys close by, so she ran round the city streets until she found it, but again the flowers were sold out except for a limp packet of tulips with a yellow reduced sticker on it. By now, it was seven thirty and she was no closer to finding a bouquet. She stood outside the supermarket and then decided she had no choice but to go to the cemetery. She couldn't actually believe that pinching flowers from graves even entered her mind, but she was desperate.

She ran to the cemetery. The headstones from those who had been cremated were situated close together so she decided if she just pinched one flower from several plots, they wouldn't be missed and she would apologise to each one as she did it. Luckily, it was beginning to get dark so there shouldn't be anyone else around. She was out of breath when she arrived. It took a couple of minutes to compose herself before beginning her mission. She jumped from one small headstone to another quickly pinching a flower from each plot that had flowers on them. All the time she was looking to see if anyone was around. As she turned her head when she thought she heard someone, she tripped over a small raised headstone. Clutching the flowers in her left hand, she put her right hand down to try and save herself. She caught the palm of that hand on the corner of the next headstone.

'Damn and blast,' she shouted out.

She looked down at her trousers and saw there was a small rip in the knee. She rolled up her trouser leg and noticed she had grazed her knee. Whilst she was studying her knee, she felt a pain in her right hand. She looked at her hand and noticed a small gash. She hadn't got time to do anything about her minor injuries, so she carried on until she felt she had enough stems to make up a bouquet. Once she had enough, she ran to the bins. The bins in the cemetery were for old tributes to be disposed of. Luckily, they didn't look like they had been emptied recently, so she ought to get what she needed from them. She rummaged around one until she found some cellophane. She chuckled to herself as it reminded her of her previous career working as a refuse collector. During that time she took some more driving qualifications, then applied for the job as a chauffeur. She had fond memories of life 'on the bins.' She wasn't one of the brightest pupils at school so was convinced she was far more intelligent these days, thanks to that job. After all, look how intelligent she was sorting out the bouquet? She considered herself to be a 'genius' with problem solving skills. It didn't occur to her that if she was that 'intelligent' she would have remembered to order the bouquet in the first place.

Josephine found a patch of grass, sat down and then began to arrange the flowers into some kind of bouquet. She realised she hadn't got a ribbon, so leapt up and ran back to the bins. She leant further and further into the bin, using the uninjured left hand to search for anything that felt remotely like ribbon… then the worst happened… she fell in head first. Whilst inside, she grabbed a piece of what she thought might be ribbon, then attempted to haul herself out. It was now fully dark, so once out of the bin, she ran with the 'ribbon' back to the grass and carried on with her bouquet making.

Suddenly, and out of the blue, there was a loud noise, a big bang.

'Noooo, noooo, not thunder, please don't rain as well, noooo.'

A big flash of lightning lit up the sky, a clear fork of it. Josephine did what you shouldn't do, grabbed her stuff and ran to shelter under the nearest tree. Whilst there was a short, sharp burst of rain, Josephine managed to carry on. She was getting on well until she picked up one flower and to her dismay it was artificial, she would have no choice but to put that one in the bin. The rain stopped, she leapt up and ran to the bin with the artificial flower. When she ran back on the wet grass, her feet went from under her and she fell flat on her bottom. She quickly recovered, stood up and wiped her wet trousers. She had to move quickly as she only had half an hour to get the 'bouquet' to the dignitary.

She managed to get the flowers arranged with the cellophane over them. She picked up the 'ribbon' and realised in the dim lights from the lamps in the cemetery, that it wasn't ribbon, it was a red shoelace.

'For goodness sake, how did a shoelace end up in the bin? And who on earth has red shoelaces?' she thought despairingly.

She had no choice but to tie the cellophane and stems together with the red shoelace. Her only consolation was that the bouquet was nice and sturdy, now it was all pulled together.

When she had finished, she put her hands together, closed her eyes and said a silent prayer to those who she had pinched a flower from, then she ran as fast as she could back to Charlie and the limousines.

Charlie was relieved to see her, although horrified to see the state she was in.

"I've looked after Bon Jovi, I gave him some water in the tupperware dish you left for him and he had a tiddle up the tree."

Josephine wasn't impressed that Bon Jovi had been drinking from her 'left overs' box, but Charlie had done a great job.

"Cheers pal, you're a star," Josephine replied to Charlie, patting him on his back.

Josephine took Bon Jovi from Charlie and put him into the bag in the front of the Jag. She flattened her hair, straightened up her suit and ran inside with the bouquet. She entered the room following the instructions she had been given and stood in her allotted place. The attendees had finished their lavish spread and had coffee cups in front of them at their tables. Josephine crossed one leg over the other leg with the hole in the knee of her trousers. She looked closely at the 'bouquet' and thought she had done a reasonable job. The cellophane was slightly crumpled, but nevermind. Right on cue, she moved a couple of steps forward, attempting to walk with one leg over the leg with the ripped trousers. The bouquet was resting over her right arm and she passed it to the dignitary with her uninjured hand, making sure that she immediately put her right arm next to her side so her injured hand wasn't on show. The dignitary gave her a stern look, which she returned with a smile. He didn't look amused. She slowly shuffled back and stood in place whilst the dignitary presented the bouquet to the royal guest.

Josephine smiled until, to her horror she noticed a small label hanging off the bottom of the bouquet. 'Jeeeez, that must be a label from a tribute, it must have been on the cellophane.'

Josephine knew she had to get that label removed.

Once the presentations were over and people were mingling, Josephine shuffled over to the bouquet which had been placed on a nearby table. She hovered around and somehow, despite her injured hand, managed to discreetly remove the label. She shoved it in her pocket. She wasn't required any further until her dignitary was ready to leave so she made her way back outside to the civic car.

Charlie was still hanging around outside.

"I left a label on the cellophane Charlie, it's in my pocket, I had to get it off without being seen."

Charlie was roaring with laughter.

"You are crazy, Josephine... Anyway, what does the card say?"

Josephine removed it from her pocket.

Remembering Great Aunt Margaret
You were our very own princess
Rest in Peace
Your loving family xxx

Josephine was horrified, there was even a royal word used in the tribute. Imagine if the royal guest had read it. She shuddered and pushed it into Charlie's hand.

"Throw it away, you muppet, I can't take it anymore. I'm going to see Rich, the chef, and see if he has any leftovers."

She picked up the tupperware box off the floor and the lid from inside the car, emptied out the leftover water that Bon Jovi hadn't drunk and went to the kitchen, where Rich filled her tub with delicious food. She put the tub on the floor in the car, next to the bag with Bon Jovi inside.

An hour later, Josephine opened the back door of the car to her dignitary, using her left hand, instead of her right. He glanced at Josephine and raised his eyebrows but didn't speak.

She set off on the ten minute journey home. She was struggling to hold the wheel properly because of the pain coming from her right palm. She was just thankful that gear changes were done with her left hand, otherwise it might have been impossible to drive back.

Five minutes into the journey, a pungent smell filled the car. She looked in the mirror and could see the dignitary pulling a face.

"Jospehine, there is an awful smell in the car, can you open your window please."

Josephine felt herself go hot, the smell was what she would describe as 'rank.' She opened the window, glanced at the car clock, only three minutes to go. She put her foot down further on the accelerator and slightly exceeded the speed limit. With just a minute to go, Bon Jovi let out another bark. Josephine began singing, "and a woof, woof here, a woof, woof there, here a woof, there a woof, everywhere a woof woof…"

She glanced at the mirror and saw the dignitary shaking his head in disbelief. Finally, Josephine pulled up outside the dignitary's home. She leapt out and opened the back door with her left hand. The dignitary climbed out of the car, looked at Josephine raising his eyebrows once again.

"Goodnight Jospehine, I think you need a good night's sleep."

"Yes Sir, of course Sir."

The dignitary quickly walked to his front door, turning around when he got there to look back at the car, shaking his head.

Josephine quickly drove off as fast as she could, back to base. As soon as she parked up the car, she went around to the passengers side. On the floor was an empty tupperware tub. Bon Jovi had eaten all the leftovers which she was going to eat before she went to bed. The smell must have been Bon Jovi passing wind, caused by the rich food he had eaten.

As soon as Josephine walked into her home, she flopped on the settee, Bon Jovi jumped on top of her. She studied her injured hand and knee.

"Jeeezz, what a day Bon Jovi… I feel like I have been living on a prayer today… Or maybe living on a wing and a prayer… or maybe saying a prayer of forgiveness."

Josephine's stomach rumbled, she looked in her food cupboard, there was nothing in it.

Bon Jovi licked her face, smiled at her and shut his eyes, full up and content.

Oh well, tomorrow is another day in the world of Josephine Blunderbus…crazy chauffeur!

For Jo!

Ferns

—⚋—

MEGAN SIGHED AS she trimmed up the fern in her back garden. She had only trimmed it a couple of weeks ago and wondered if it literally grew several inches overnight. There were other smaller ferns dotted about the garden but as they were still small she decided to leave them for now. The main thing was that she had sorted out the massive one which was just too much for the size of the garden.

"Mum, mum, where are you?" Megan smiled and walked to the back door where Lizzie, her fourteen year old daughter had just walked in through the front door.

"I got home from work early, so I just went fern chopping," she replied to Lizzie.

Megan went to the sink to wash her dirty hands and asked Lizzie what kind of a day she had.

"It was okay, mum. Can we go to Old Mother Shipton's Cave sometime?"

Megan dried her hands and turned to Lizzie.

"We can ask dad when he gets home and see what he thinks. It's not that far from here. What makes you want to go there Lizzie?"

"I saw a programme and they showed the objects hanging up, which turn to stone by the water from the well."

Later on that day, the family sat down in the kitchen for their evening meal. Lizzie's older brother Sam was as usual teasing Lizzie, with dad, Rob, attempting to keep the peace between them.

Megan brought up Lizzie's request to visit Knaresborough where Old Mother Shipton's Cave was situated. She had been thinking about it whilst preparing the evening meal. They deserved some time off, she thought. They had only been living in their period cottage for six months and had spent most of their spare time decorating or tidying the overgrown garden. Megan and Rob had always wanted to move from their suburban home to the country but were worried about uprooting the children. Sam, a bubbly teenager, the life and soul of parties, wasn't too worried because he only had another year at school and then off to university. Lizzie was studious, thoughtful, loved social history and old buildings and adored living in an old cottage. Both children now had to walk to the end of the lane to pick up a bus for school, whereas they could walk from their old home. The cottage had been empty for several months when the family had viewed it. There had been an elderly lady living there but she had passed away so her family sold it.

Sam pulled a face at the suggestion of the outing.

"Sounds boring, I'm not going." he said. Rob laughed at him.

"Okay Sam, you can stay here! Why don't the three of us stay overnight and make a weekend of it? All we have done is work since we moved in. It will do us good, as long as Sam doesn't arrange any parties here whilst we are gone!"

"As if!" Sam replied. "Who wants to party out here? Can't wait to get to uni so I can party properly."

"Good, I'm glad you're not coming Sam, it will be great without you," Lizzie pulled a face at Sam.

"Well that's settled then," Rob said. "I'll get on my laptop later and book us a night somewhere when we've sorted out a suitable weekend."

Megan smiled and thought how nice it would be to go and relax, maybe have an evening meal out, in fact a weekend of little cooking.

One Saturday morning, two weeks later Rob, Megan and Lizzie checked in at a guest house overlooking the River Nidd. The weather was beautiful, the three of them were in good spirits and excited about the trip. They weren't able to go to their room which was a double room with a door leading to a separate bedroom for Lizzie. The room would be ready at two o'clock, so they just parked up, left their bags and arranged to come back later on.

The three of them spent the rest of the morning walking around, they stood at the viaduct looking down on the most spectacular scenery. Houses and guest houses lined one side of the river with Old Mother Shipton's Cave opposite.

They had brought a picnic lunch so they found suitable bench type seating to enjoy their lunch before going to Mother Shiptons. Rob was holding the cool box so once settled he opened it up and passed around the sandwiches, bags of crisps, fruit and bottles of juice. They chatted happily whilst they ate, then Rob gave Sam a call to let him know they had got there and what it was like so far.

Whilst Rob was chatting to Sam, Megan and Lizzie sat on the bench looking around. Megan laughed.

"What are you laughing at mum?"

"Just the overgrown fern in front of us, it just reminds me of home and how quickly they spread and grow. Almost like they grow six inches overnight!"

Lizzie walked over to it, then bent down next to it.

"What are you doing Lizzie?

Lizzie didn't answer but walked back to Megan holding something.

"When I looked down at the fern, I saw this, and wondered what it was so I picked it up."

Her hand was clasped, but when Lizzie opened it, Megan saw a tarnished heart shaped small locket. There was no chain with it.

"Does it open, Lizzie?"

Lizzie sat down next to Megan and opposite Rob who had finished talking to Sam, but then had taken a call to do with his work. Rob was self employed, so work never went away even for holidays. Once Lizzie had released the clasp and opened it, they looked at the black and white pictures. One side was a picture of a young lady's face and the other side was a baby's face.

"Ahh that's nice." Lizzie exclaimed. "A mum and her baby."

"Yes, it is," Megan replied. "But nothing you can do with it love, because we don't know who it belongs to and by the looks of it, it is very old and looks like it has been lost for ages. It's a wonder you even spotted it. I would just leave it here, it's dirty anyway."

Megan stood up, then gathered up the rubbish and placed it in a bin not far away from where they sat, whilst Lizzie, after studying the pictures in the locket again, closed it back up.

The three of them headed towards the entrance of Mother Shipton's Cave where they spent the afternoon. They visited the cave and stood looking at all the hanging items which had turned to stone under the water from the well pouring over them. Lizzie was fascinated with different objects and watched for quite some time until Rob suggested they walk along the side of the river before heading back to the guest house.

The three of them had a good hearty meal in a local pub that evening and all enjoyed a peaceful night's sleep before waking up early to a beautiful sunny morning. They were all full up after the large English breakfasts they had eaten, before checking out of the guest house.

Rob suggested they have a short walk to take in the magnificent view over the river before going on to Harrogate for the final few hours of the weekend break. None of them could manage any more food after the big breakfast, so after a few hours sightseeing, they went to a coffee shop for some drinks.

Later on, they headed home to prepare a simple evening meal with Sam, who hadn't had a cooked meal since the last one they had together on Friday evening. Megan noticed that the loaf of bread she had left Sam was nearly gone as well as the large block of Red Leicester cheese. The first thing she did after noticing the sandwich supplies had diminished was to get another loaf from the freezer in the hope that it defrosted enough to be able to make sandwiches for pack ups the next day.

The family sat down during the evening and chatted about the weekend, telling Sam all about it.

"Glad, I didn't go," Sam laughed. "Sounds like you had a good time though."

The next few weeks flew by with everyone busy as usual. Megan carried on doing as much as she could in the garden before it started to become cooler as autumn arrived. There were some decorating jobs still to be finished during the winter months.

One afternoon when Megan returned from work, she decided to see how much loft space there was. Rob had put a ladder up there which pulled down and so far they had not stored anything up there. He had also put some lighting up there. As they had thrown out a lot of items when they moved including old Christmas decorations, Megan had made up her mind to buy new ones including a nice artificial tree, all of which would be stored in the loft.

She also decided to put a couple of suitcases up there because they wouldn't be used again until the following year. She took each suitcase up the steps and put them next to the hatch entrance inside the loft, then she went inside the loft. She decided to move the suitcases to a corner of the loft space. The loft had already got flooring down which must have been done by the previous owners. She moved them one at a time, then just as she was ready to go down the steps, she noticed something in the opposite corner to where she had put the cases. She couldn't make out what it was. The lighting that Rob had set up was fairly dim so she walked over and when looking close up, she found a small, old carrier bag. Tentatively, she opened the bag. Inside were a few ornaments which must have just been left by the previous occupants. She picked one out and it looked like a seaside ornament, she delved in further and picked out an ornamental egg cup. She decided that from what she had seen there was nothing of any great expense, just a bag of ornaments that were probably given to the couple from family members' holidays.

Megan took the bag out of the loft and when she went downstairs, put it next to an armchair in the lounge with the intention of going through it to establish if there was anything of value or sentimental value. If there was, then they would have to contact their solicitor.

Lizzie came in from school.

"What's for tea mum," she asked.

"Not sure love, I've been busy since I got back from work. Maybe we can have some pasta. I've got some garlic bread in the freezer."

The four of them sat down to a meal of pasta, salad and garlic bread at the kitchen table later that evening. Once they had all cleared away, Sam went off to his mates house and Lizzie sat and watched a TV soap with Megan. Rob went upstairs to the corner of the bedroom which he had turned into a mini office area, to complete some paperwork. Something he did most weekday evenings for an hour or so.

Once the soap had finished, Megan and Lizzie chatted about the Christmas decorations they plan to buy.

"If we start buying some bits soon, we can store them in the loft until we put them up at the beginning of December," Megan said to Lizzie.

"Good idea mum, let's make our first Christmas here fun and put loads of decorations and lights up," Lizzie replied excitedly.

"Oh yes Lizzie, that's just reminded me, let's have a look at those trinkets in the bag I found in the loft."

Megan put her hand down next to her chair and picked up the bag. She also picked up the newspaper left on the settee from when Rob had read it and spread it on the floor because the bag looked grubby. She picked out the items and both of them looked at them. Rob came back downstairs having finished his paperwork and asked what they were doing. He picked up the TV remote and put a programme on he wanted to watch.

Megan put out the first few items onto the newspaper and it did seem that they were seaside ornaments, probably just kept up in the loft because the elderly couple had not wanted to discard them. Lizzie sat on the floor pulling faces at some of the tacky ornaments, some of which named the seaside resorts.

Megan put the rest of what was in the bag onto the newspaper and there was also an old book and a small photo album.

Megan looked at the book which was about Cornish coasts and Lizzie flicked through the photo album. It was very old and some pages just had "stick on" photo corners, with the photos missing. They had probably dropped out over the years. There was the odd photo still attached.

Lizzie put the book down and said to Megan she was going upstairs to the toilet. Megan raised her eyebrows then carried on looking at the book.

When Lizzie returned, some ten minutes later, she sat down again on the floor next to the newspaper.

"Mum there's something strange I am going to say."

Megan looked up from the book and Rob turned towards Lizzie, away from the programme he had been engrossed in.

"I was just looking at this old photo album. Then I found a couple of loose photos at the back, which had probably dropped out of the corners. One was of a couple, with the lady holding a baby and two older children standing each side of them, then there was another one."

Rob sighed.

"Oh Lizzie, I thought you were going to say something interesting." He turned his head back to the programme he had been watching.

"It is interesting dad, because the other one had the lady's and the baby's heads cut out."

Rob just raised his eyebrows and carried on watching TV, whilst Megan looked down at the book.

"Look mum and dad, the lady whose head was missing was in another family photo and so was the baby and they are the couple in the locket."

"Lizzie, for goodness sake, I want to watch this programme… what are you talking about? What locket?" Rob looked exasperated.

Megan decided to intervene.

"Lizzie found a locket when we were in Knaresborough, Rob. You were on the phone at the time." She then turned to Lizzie.

"But Lizzie I still don't know what you are talking about because you left the locket on the picnic table. It was dirty and there was nothing we could do with it."

"No mum, I bought it home and gave it a clean. I sometimes look at it because I felt there was a story with it. Most people would have their partner or spouse on the other side. I didn't tell you because you would have told me to put it down, I just stuffed it in my pocket."

Megan and Rob just looked at Lizzie.

"Okay Lizzie, fetch the locket and show us what you mean." Megan instructed her.

Rob, by now was feeling grumpy and turned back to the TV again. Lizzie ran upstairs and brought down the locket. She opened it up and then got the photo album and took out the two photos. She showed her mum and dad the family photo and then the photo with the two heads missing.

Rob and Megan just stared in amazement as they both realised that Lizzie was right.

It went quiet for a few seconds until Rob broke the silence.

"All we can do is contact our solicitor and mention we still have some property from the previous owner and can they make contact with the family of the previous owner's solicitor. Nothing more we can do apart from put the locket in the bag too. It's no use saying where the locket was found, it's not necessary. It can just go in the bag with the ornaments. It's over to them then. Mind you, well done our Lizzie! You little detective! I still can't believe it, but you are most definitely right!"

"But dad, I want to know why the lady was with the baby in the locket. That's why I bought the locket home. I just used to look at it and wonder and my theory is that the baby died."

"Oh how sad." Megan said to Lizzie. "I can see why you think that, particularly as you have found a photo and they seem to be a family of five. So you would naturally expect the man and woman to be in the locket, but we will never know. Let's just hope you are wrong. Maybe the baby was a girl? It's hard to tell with the baby being dressed in a christening gown. Clearly the other two older children were boys. So could be a mother and daughter locket. Let's think that scenario, rather than the other."

They packed the items back into the bag and Megan found a jewellery box to put the locket in so it didn't get lost. It was then placed into the bag.

Eventually, the bag went to the solicitor's to deal with and although Lizzie was sorry to see the locket go, she felt happy in the knowledge that it will hopefully reach the family.

The weeks passed by and Christmas was drawing near. Megan and Lizzie had bought lots of decorations as well as an artificial tree, all of which were stored in the loft, ready to be brought out at the beginning of December.

When the time came, the family arranged to get the cottage looking festive on a Saturday three weeks before Christmas. Sam was not interested and went out with his friend. Rob planned to go outside into the front garden and set up some Christmas lights in the Mountain Ash tree with Megan and Lizzie decorating inside. Lizzie put on Christmas tunes and was happy sorting out the lights for the tree which Megan had put up in the corner of their cosy lounge.

The front door opened and Rob shouted, "We have a visitor." He walked in the lounge with a man, who was probably in his sixties, holding a large box of chocolates. Megan and Lizzie looked up and smiled at the stranger.

"This is Mike," Rob said. "He has come to thank us for the bag." Megan smiled but wasn't sure what Rob was talking about.

"My name is Mike Thorpe and I just want to thank you so much for taking the trouble to return my parent's possessions which had been left behind here. It was very kind of you."

Megan smiled when she realised what he was talking about.

"You are very welcome."

"As you probably saw, a lot of what was in the bag is seaside ornaments. My mother just wouldn't part with them as we… meaning me and my younger brother, used to bring these things back from holidays as most people did years ago! The book, well I'm so pleased to get that back for sentimental reasons and it's great to get the mini photo album although I know some of the photo's had been mislaid over the years."

Lizzie listened, intrigued. She was just willing him to mention the locket and say what happened to the baby.

"We are so pleased we could help Mike." Megan smiled at him whilst he continued.

"Thing is, I'm just stunned by the locket. I couldn't believe my eyes when I opened the box. Mum and Dad went on a day trip to Knaresborough and Harrogate several years ago and mum was devastated when she got home and found the locket had dropped off during the day, leaving her with just an empty chain around her neck. She had been wearing a scarf and several times during the day she had taken it off and put it back on again so she thought she must have caught it with that. How on earth did it end up in a box in that bag?"

"Lizzie, you can tell Mike!" Rob said, looking at Lizzie. He gestured to Mike to sit down even though the lounge was scattered with Christmas decorations. Mike placed the chocolates onto the coffee table then listened to Lizzie who relayed the whole story to him. Mike sat smiling and shaking his head in amazement. Lizzie just looked at him, waiting for all to be revealed. Soon the suspense was over as Mike found his voice and carried on.

"Wow, that is amazing. The reason why my mum was so distraught is that the baby in the locket is our sister. My father was in the forces and stationed in Germany for a time when Stephen, my brother and I were young kids. Mum struggled on her own and had an affair which resulted in our sister being born. When dad came home, he was shocked but after he calmed down he accepted her and she was baptised. The two photos you found were the only two taken that day. Not long after the christening, dad found he could not cope with bringing up another man's baby so he made mum give her up. We can vaguely remember it happening at the time. Mum obviously was distraught, but had to cope because she had no choice."

Mike looked sad. Lizzie felt some relief in the knowledge that the baby hadn't died but also a feeling of sadness at the poor woman having to give up her only daughter. Mike continued.

"My father was very strict and was some years older than my mum. After the shame of the neighbours knowing and gossiping, dad sold the house and bought this cottage and we started a new life without our sister and it was as if she had never existed. Mum never mentioned her whilst dad was alive, but she kept the locket around her neck all the time. It made her feel close to our sister. Dad always thought there was a picture of both of them in the locket and assumed she was so upset about losing it because he had bought the locket for her. He was never aware of the baby's picture in it. She eventually lost the chain too but wasn't so concerned about that, just distraught about the locket."

Lizzie was beginning to feel choked up but managed to compose herself. Mike sighed then carried on.

"I'm so sorry, I'm keeping you from your decorating. Have to say the cottage looks wonderful. It had gone down the last few years mum was here. We did what we could but there was only so much time we could spend here."

Lizzie was feeling frustrated now because she wanted Mike to finish the story, not talk about the cottage.

"It's no problem Mike." Rob said. "You just carry on, but can I make you a coffee? We could all do with one."

"That would be great, thanks Rob, I take it black with no sugar."

Rob went to the kitchen and soon came back with four mugs of steaming coffee. After some general chit chat, Mike carried on with his story.

"My father passed away suddenly about a year after the bus trip where mum had lost the locket. Sometime after, mum talked to Stephen and me about our sister. There had been no mention of her whilst my father had been alive. Stephen and I had discussed her alot with our families and we always hoped she had a good life. But between us and with dad gone we knew we had to find her. To cut a long story short, we eventually found our lovely half sister and Joanne and mum were finally reunited."

Lizzie finally felt relief. She looked at Megan and smiled. Mike sipped his coffee, then carried on.

"They had a few good years seeing each other before mum sadly passed away, and mum had been so happy, particularly in the knowledge that Joanne had had a great upbringing and had never felt the need to look for her birth parents because she loved her adoptive parents. Mum met Joanne's family and we see Joanne on a regular basis. Mum probably hid the photo album in the bag in the loft and I'm sorry it hadn't been moved with the rest of the things after mum died. We had a clearance firm to clear the unwanted belongings and they must have missed that bag. Now I have the locket, I want to give it to Joanne, so I can't thank Lizzie enough for finding it and taking it home."

"I probably speak for all of us Mike, but we are so pleased the clearance company missed it! Also I'm not surprised they did, it was tucked in a corner." Megan said. "We are so thrilled your mum spent time with her daughter and Lizzie will be very relieved that the "baby" is alive!"

They all chatted for a while longer until Mike stood up to leave.

Mike looked at Lizzie and then suggested that perhaps she would like to meet Joanne sometime. After he had said that to her, it came to him that maybe Lizzie could be there when he gave Joanne the locket, then she could relay the story to her. They exchanged numbers and Mike left.

Soon after the family sat at the table and ate their lunch where they discussed Mike's visit. Lizzie was just delighted that the baby had not died and relieved to know the story behind the locket. She was also looking forward to meeting Joanne in the future.

Once lunch was over and they had cleared up. Megan suggested that she and Lizzie go out into the back garden whilst it was still light, decorate some bushes and put some solar lights in the ground. They could finish inside later when it got dark, later in the afternoon. Megan fetched the box of lights and they both wrapped up warmly and went out into the garden. Lizzie picked up a small string of lights, suitable for outside with a small battery pack and placed them around a bush next to the small fern, one that had not been butchered by her mum! She was happy rearranging the string, trying to make them look great and also feeling Christmassy.

After a while, Megan who was at the other side of the garden looked round at Lizzie, who by then was kneeling down looking at something.

"What are you doing Lizzie? You will get damp trousers kneeling on the grass."

Lizzie didn't look up, so Megan went over to her.

"Mum, I've just found this in the small fern whilst I was putting the lights on the bush."

Lizzie held up a dirty chain which was broken.

"Is this the chain which held the locket, mum?"

"It could be, all Mike said is that the chain eventually was lost. There's every possibility that the chain could have been lost in the garden. Why don't we just clean it up later?"

Lizzie took it inside and then the two of them carried on with their decorating.

Later that evening after they had eaten their supper, all pleased with their beautifully decorated country cottage, looking so festive, Lizzie fetched the chain. Megan cleaned it up and Rob looked at it. The chain was broken.

"There is a possibility that the chain did hold the locket. There was a tiny loop on the chain which could have held the locket. The loop has a small opening in it, where the locket could have been pulled through when Mike's mum removed her scarf on the day out and the locket may have just dropped to the floor without her knowing. I think we should take it to the jewellers and get it cleaned up and repaired. It's a nice chain."

They all agreed that was the best thing to do.

Soon Christmas Eve came around. The family spent the day preparing for Christmas Day, well all of them except Sam. He had gone into town with his mates deciding that would be more exciting than being in the countryside. The weather was sunny with a blue cloudless sky. If you looked up to the sky, vapour trails could be seen coming from the aeroplanes flying over.

The phone rang and Rob answered it in the lounge. He came into the kitchen where Megan and Lizzie were, grinning.

"That was Mike. He asked if he could pop round just to wish us a nice Christmas. He is coming in about twenty minutes. I'm glad he rang because we have that chain back from the jewellers, all cleaned up, repaired and in a nice box. I thought because we had been so busy, it would be next year before we could give it to him."

Mike turned up at the time expected. He bought a gift bag for the family and a separate gift for Lizzie. He put the presents on the coffee table.

"I've actually got Joanne in the car."

"Please bring her in Mike, we would love to meet her."

She was a lovely, pleasant lady who got on well with the family and chatted excitedly about how she was so pleased that she had been 'found' by the family. After about twenty minutes and conscious of the time, Mike removed the box containing the locket from his pocket. Lizzie relayed the story to Joanne who was just stunned by it all. Once she had admired the locket, Rob then decided that the time was right to bring up the chain.

Rob removed the box from his pocket, opened the box up and handed it to Joanne. Lizzie explained her latest 'find'. Joanne was so moved, she had tears in her eyes. Mike smiled, shaking his head in amazement. Megan felt a lump in her throat and looked at Lizzie who's bottom lip was quivering. Joanne quickly recovered and looked around at them all.

"I am just totally speechless, thank you all so much, especially you Lizzie. This means more to me than any other Christmas present. I will feel so close to mum all the time with this on.

Joanne put the locket on the loop of the chain and squeezed it together so it didn't drop off ever again. She then put the necklace on with some assistance from her brother.

Just as Mike had finished doing up the clasp, they all went quiet because they could hear voices.

"Silent night, holy night…"

Rob went to the door and there was a choir outside carol singing. The rest of them followed and went outside to listen to the choir. The choir were collecting for a local children's hospice so Megan popped back indoors to fetch some money to put in their bucket.

Joanne put her arm around Lizzie's shoulder as the choir sang… "sleep in heavenly peace".

She whispered to Lizzie.

"Have a lovely Christmas, Lizzie…you have certainly made mine."

Hidden Disabilities- Story

A Bag for Life

—ɯ—

This chapter is about Hidden Disabilities, which thankfully has been highlighted over recent years, which is good news.

How many times have you heard the comment: 'That person shouldn't be using the disabled toilet' or 'Why have they got a Blue Badge?'

Hopefully, with more recognition of hidden disabilities, society will learn to be less judgemental, because none of us know what is going on in another's mind or what may be underneath their clothes.

The story is about Katie living with a stoma. It is estimated that around 1 in 500 people live with a stoma (Colostomy UK, 2019), some permanent and some temporary. A stoma can be for a Colostomy, Ileostomy or Urostomy. I really hope this has not put you off and you move onto the next chapter without reading it! I can assure you that the story is not about wee or poo!

The two verses following on from the story really just speak for themselves.

"I'm afraid we will have to operate and you will have a permanent stoma," the Consultant looked at a shocked Katie. A few minutes later Katie, holding her husband Chris's hand, replied;

"If that's what keeps me from dying and gives me longer with Chris and my family, that's fine."

The Consultant raised his eyebrows, probably in amazement that Katie remained so matter of fact about the shock news.

"Will I lose my hair if I have to have chemotherapy afterwards?" she added.

The MacMillan nurse sitting opposite her smiled, maybe with amusement that Katie was probably more concerned about losing her naturally blonde hair, which would grow back, than having a stoma. She joined in with the conversation.

"Let's not worry about that yet, you may not need chemotherapy."

"Okay, that's fine, what happens next?" Katie looked at the Consultant, then the MacMillan nurse for more information.

Over the next few weeks it was a whirl of scans and appointments leading up to operation. The operation was then followed by gruelling treatments. Katie had no problems adjusting to life with a colostomy, but more importantly, the treatments did not result in any hair loss!

Over the following years, Katie recovered as much as she could and family and working life resumed.

Her first recollection of 'bags' was when she was a young child. She had barged into a spare bedroom at her home forgetting that a relative was stopping over, only to find him changing his bag. Back then the stigma of 'having a bag' was far greater than in more recent times. At her age then, she didn't know anything about them and it played on her mind sometimes by what she had seen. It was made worse by the fact that she ran out the room straight to her mum downstairs and said she was frightened. Her mum put her finger over her mouth:

"Shush Katie, go outside and play."

Back then, things like that were brushed under the carpet. Thankfully, things had improved over time. For many years, prior to Katie having her operation, she had always supported the Crohns and Colitis Bluebell Walk each year, because one of her friends had an Ileostomy. David was always pleased when Katie and her family joined him and Paula for the charity walk. So Katie knew people who had 'bags' which is probably why she was able to cope better with the news she was to have one. Not once had Katie thought 'why me?'

Over the years, the one thing that did annoy her was when she heard people talking about others who had stoma's. A common comment might be, "Did you know (so and so) has a bag now?" or "Don't you feel sorry for (so and so) they have a bag."

Katie had now lived with her bag for five years. In all that time she had not felt at all sorry for herself so why should other people feel sorry for her? Maybe all those other thousands of people who had permanent or temporary bags didn't want sympathy? Infact Katie had spent a lot of time thinking about the time when she may have said she feels sorry for so and so. Did that person want others to feel sorry for them? Probably not. She had also done a lot of thinking about disabilities and hidden disabilities. In some ways Katie wished she had made a career in some kind of health care work. But, it was too late now, she had spent her working life in retail and it was probably too late to change her career particularly as it would cost a lot of money to retrain, and she needed to earn money to help with the bills, not spend it on herself. Having thought of what might have been, she did, though, enjoy her job at the large department store in the city. She had several good friends in her department which was a branded clothing section.

When Katie returned to work after her operation, her bosses were very supportive and made 'reasonable adjustments' to her change of circumstances, which made her feel very comfortable at work. She worked three long days each week, including one day at the weekend, alternate Saturdays and Sundays. Apart from her bosses and a couple of work colleagues who she worked closely with, no-one else at work was aware of her colostomy. There was no need for anyone else to know. Katie didn't keep it a secret, but she didn't broadcast it either.

One day at work, Katie went to the canteen for her fifteen minute break. It was just after eleven o'clock and the canteen was pretty full. She didn't see anyone she knew really well so she sat on the only empty chair she could see at the end of a long table. The department store was very big, with lots of staff all working different shifts. There were a lot of staff that she saw around, but apart from acknowledging with a friendly 'hi' to, she didn't even know many of their names.

She was sipping her coffee whilst replying to a text message from her daughter, when she overheard a conversation between two staff members, sitting two seats away from her, neither of whom Katie knew.

"Do you know when Kay is coming back, Helen?"

"No, I spoke to her husband and he thinks it could be a month or so," replied the one called Helen.

"I heard she is having 'a bag', that sounds horrible, bet she won't be able to come back with one of those," said the one whose name she didn't know. The two women both pulled a face.

The conversation struck a raw nerve with Katie who was normally fairly quiet and reserved. Suddenly, she stood up and looked at both of them and what came out of her mouth surprised herself, not to mention Helen, her colleague and others in the canteen.

"I have what you call 'a bag', if I didn't have 'a bag' I would be dead."

The whole canteen went quiet and Katie felt herself blush, she grabbed her bag and headed to the loos. Once inside, she sprinkled some cold water on her hot face, nipped into a cubicle for a wee, then washed her hands, composed herself and went back to her section. She tried to put the whole incident out of her mind, despite how hard it was. Thank goodness she wasn't back to work until the weekend.

The following couple of days where she was either busy at home or shopping, her mind kept returning to the incident in the canteen. She had mentioned it to Chris whilst they were having their tea one night and his reply was, 'Good for you!'

It was so out of character for her to speak up like that. She felt bad about eavesdropping into their conversation but conversely they spoke so loud and it was offensive, particularly the way they pulled faces at each other. To make matters worse they were chatting about their 'friend' and work colleague's personal business and who had clearly been through such a lot. So much was going on in her mind and for once she was not looking forward to going in to work on her next working day, to a job that she usually loved.

When she did go back, it was business as usual and she soon got into the normal routine. She was also worried about bumping into the ladies who she had stood up to. When it reached late morning, her boss rang down and requested to have a word with her in the office at two o'clock. Katie decided to go out at lunchtime for a walk, she felt anxious about the meeting. When it reached two o'clock a nervous Katie knocked on her bosses door. "Come in."

Katie walked in and to her surprise the two members of staff who made the comments in the canteen were sitting on chairs next to her bosses desk, both looking a little sheepish. Her boss swivelled her chair around and welcomed Katie.

"Katie, Helen and Julia have something to say to you."

Helen turned to the side of the chair and picked up a beautiful flower arrangement and presented it to Katie.

"Both Julia and myself are so very sorry, Katie. We were out of order discussing the personal business of our friend and work colleague. We didn't realise how hurtful we were being and we should have, we are deeply ashamed."

Julia didn't speak but looked close to tears.

"You are both forgiven," a shocked Katie replied. "Let's just forget about it and learn from it. I have already because I shouldn't have been eavesdropping on your conversation. Thanks so much for the flowers, they are beautiful."

With that, the two ladies left the office, leaving Katie with her boss.

"Sit down Katie, I want a quick chat," she said.

Katie sat down in one of the now vacant chairs.

"Katie, one staff member reported to me what happened and what you said. Thank you for accepting their apology, but there is one thing I want to ask you. Obviously, I knew you had a stoma and I hope you don't mind me bringing it up?"

"No not at all, it's not a secret, but just something I don't go round broadcasting…well not normally!" Katie laughed.

"Well I wondered if you would consider this? We are in the process of doing our new promotions brochure. How do you feel about modelling some sportswear with another staff member from our London store? He, like yourself, has a stoma. There are new lines of sports wear that are suitable for people with stomas and hernias."

"Wow, I like the thought of being a model especially if it raises awareness. Anything that reduces the stigma of a stoma can only be good." Katie smiled. "I also think that I will treat myself to some fancy unique cover for my bag!"

"There is an added bonus, Katie, you will be paid quite well for it too!"

They both laughed.

Katie went back to her section. Her worries lifted. She smiled to herself, just amused at the thought of modelling sportswear!

She couldn't wait to get home and announce her new second job to the family over their planned takeaway meal that evening! A Chinese takeaway that Chris would pick up and carry home in their supermarket 'bag for life' ... to Katie and her 'bag for life!'

Hidden Disabilities – Verse 1

So I look well
How do you know?
How do you know what goes on inside?
How do you know if I have a disability you can't see?
You don't because I look well.

If you do know and I need help
Maybe at work or elsewhere
Don't patronise
Just listen and try and understand
Don't listen and pretend to understand
One day it could happen to you.

Hidden Disabilities – Verse 2

Dedicated to a Health Professional

You never smiled
Now I know why
You were always immaculate
You looked and you listened
You did not miss a thing
You went above and beyond
You were a health professional
You lived under a black cloud
You were there to care, but the care was not there for you.

Who are You?

—◊—

Niamh quickly locked the front door of her flat and hurried along the parade to open up the shop where she worked. As usual, she was a few minutes late and as usual she hoped nobody would be waiting for her to unlock. Getting to places on time was not her strong point but opening a music shop a few minutes late wasn't as bad as opening a doctor's surgery a few minutes late. When she arrived she quickly switched on the lights and threw her jacket and bag on the chair in the back room. She looked out of the window at the blue sky with very few clouds and thought what a beautiful day it was. She hadn't noticed when she was walking because she was in too much of a hurry.

It was a Monday morning in the spring of 1980. The record store sold 45 rpm records, otherwise known as singles, long playing albums, cassette tapes, various musical instruments and accessories. Niamh decided she would change the display in the window that day. First, she decided to make herself a cup of tea, something that she had omitted earlier at her flat because she had not got up early enough to manage breakfast. She was twenty years old and had worked in the shop for two years. She did work with another lady for the first year, who had worked full time, but when she left, the owner replaced her with another member of staff, who worked just a few hours a week so Niamh could have some time off. Trade had slowed down over the past few years, this was down to supermarkets, some of which had begun stocking cut price records and tapes. Independent stores were finding it harder to survive. The owner had recently suggested she push sales of musical instruments, particularly the recorders for school children as well as guitars, violins and music books and stands.

Niamh placed an album on the turntable, and drank her tea. She put on a popular album which she enjoyed as she did many others. She loved all the songs on it and hoped one day to see the band in concert. Once she had finished drinking her tea, she set about removing the items out of the window and cleaning the window ready to begin a new display. A customer came in so Niamh walked to the counter and stood behind it whilst the customer browsed through the empty, long playing album covers. Finally, the customer brought the chosen album cover to the counter and Niamh searched for the matching record. All the records were neatly filed. She carefully placed the disc in the empty cover and placed the album in a bag. She took the money from the customer, had a pleasant chat and once the customer had gone went back to the window display.

Whilst she was standing in the window arranging a guitar on a stand she noticed an elderly gent stooped over, walking slowly past the shop. His head was fixed on the pavement because he was so bent over. His clothes were old and he had a small old looking dog attached to a scruffy lead walking slowly by his side. 'I wonder who he is?' she thought. 'Haven't seen him before.' The town was quite small so Niamh did recognise most people's faces as they walked by, even if she didn't know them. Anyway, she carried on with the window display until one side of the album had finished, then she popped back behind the counter to flip it over.

The morning passed quietly with very few customers until her friend Paul came in at lunchtime. He worked at the local building society but his heart was in the music shop where he had worked when he was a teenager, as a Saturday help. He came in his lunch hour every day and it gave Niamh a chance to pop to the bank with the previous trading days sales and also pick up some shopping. Paul and Niamh had a brief chat, then Niamh removed the takings from the safe in the floor and set off to the bank. Next she crossed the road and nipped to the local deli for a pate cob. Whilst walking back, she passed the elderly gent with the dog again. She felt sorry for the little dog, it looked so sad and old. She ran back into the shop and put the kettle on to make herself and Paul a drink. Paul only had about fifteen minutes left before returning to the building society. Whilst she ate her lunch she chatted to Paul.

"The number one single has gone down the charts this week," she said to him. "There are quite a lot left so I will have to send some back. I won't be very popular again at head office, but I don't have a crystal ball!"

Paul laughed with her. It was very difficult to judge the sale of the records. Niamh then changed the subject from chart topping records to telling Paul about the little old man and his sad dog. They chatted about the 'joys of getting older' whilst Paul finished his drink.

The week passed by with a steady stream of customers. It was quieter in the Spring and Summer for the sale of records and cassettes but the musical instruments and accessories helped to keep sales steady. On the Saturday, some regulars came in, including an elderly couple and their young grandson. They were the main carers of the child. Niamh knew he had a mother but gathered she had problems. They didn't have much patience with him. Niamh thought they were a bit past it to look after a child so young. Little Aaron was always singing songs, so the grandparents used to buy him a record each week. Aaron would sit on the counter and choose which one he wanted. Niamh put on the first record for him to listen to. He sang to it and Niamh thought he had such a beautiful voice.

"He has such a lovely voice," Niamh said to his grandparents who just grunted.

'What a shame,' she thought. 'He's a lovely singer for such a young child but they don't seem interested. Maybe they just get worn out looking after him at their age and don't have the energy to encourage anything that might help him with his development.'

Just as she was deep in thought, a local radio DJ walked in and stopped in his tracks when he heard little Aaron singing along to the music.

"Wow, you have a great voice for a young chap." he smiled at Aaron.

"Couldn't you have him singing on your radio show Johnny?" Niamh laughed.

Johnny then turned to the grandparents and asked them if he could record Aaron singing along to a record and incorporate it as part of his radio programme. Niamh was only joking, so she was worried what his grandparents would think, but they were fine with it, even raising a smile.

At the end of the long day, Niamh was locking up the shop when she saw the old gent with the sad looking dog walk by.

She watched them walk down the road before she set off home. After a few minutes they turned into a bungalow. When Niamh walked past the small bungalow, she saw how neglected it was. The garden was overgrown, the bungalow was in a bad state of disrepair, with cracks in the windows and a front door that looked like it would fall to bits if it were opened. 'He must have been living there a long time,' she thought. She wondered why she had not noticed him before walking by although she didn't have all day to be watching out the window, people spotting.

One Saturday morning several weeks later, little Aaron came into the shop, but this time with a younger lady and not his grandparents.

"Hello Aaron, how are you?" Niamh asked him. He smiled and the lady replied to her.

"I want to thank you," she began. Niamh wondered what on earth for?

"I'm Sadie, Aaron's aunt. As you probably know, my parents are the main carer's for Aaron." Then she explained to Niamh that Aaron was her sister's child. Niamh asked Aaron what song he wanted to listen to this week and when he had chosen, she put it on the turntable for him to sing along to.

Sadie carried on.

"Since Johnny let Aaron sing a track on his radio programme, it made my parents realise that they didn't encourage him to do anything other than go to school, so they asked me if I could arrange or him to join some activities like a singing and dance class because they don't have enough energy to do anymore. I had no idea he enjoyed singing and dancing and couldn't believe how beautiful he sang until I heard him on the radio!"

Niamh chatted to Sadie for a few more minutes in between serving other customers and then they left. When the shop went quiet for a few minutes and Niamh had time to think, she felt pleased for Aaron that he could take part in activities other than school, thanks to his Auntie Sadie.

The weeks turned to months and as winter came, the shop became busier. Over the months Niamh still noticed the old gentleman with his old dog most days, walking to the shops and back again and one thing she did notice is that he rarely carried much shopping. 'Maybe he doesn't eat much,' she thought one day.

The nights were drawing in and it was dark when she locked up the shop each night.

Life went on and just a week before Christmas, it dawned on Niamh that she had not seen the elderly gentleman for a few days. 'I hope he is well,' she thought. Later that day when she locked up in the dark, she decided to look at the old man's bungalow on the way home.

'Maybe I'm just downright nosey,' she thought. As she walked slowly by, she noticed a light was on, she could see a single light bulb dimly shining through the grubby net curtains. 'He must be alright, his light is on,' she convinced herself. She carried on walking home as quickly as she could, it was a freezing cold evening.

The next morning Niamh ran from home to the shop, only five minutes late, after making a determined effort to almost be on time because this was the busiest time of the year. She unlocked the door and there was a letter on the mat addressed to her. She put the lights on followed by the kettle, then opened the letter. It contained two tickets for a pantomime which Aaron was starring in, sent by Sadie. 'How lovely, he must have done well since Sadie took him to his dance and singing classes.' she thought. It was for a Sunday matinee performance at the end of

January. 'Not sure who I will take though, I could ask mum but then I would want to ask dad too. Mmm, I will have a think, maybe my friend Angie might want to come? Nevermind, plenty of time to think about it.'

Later that evening after she had locked up, she walked past the old gentleman's bungalow. She hadn't seen him for at least five days now. On impulse, she walked down the drive, the light was on in the front room but she decided to go around the back. When she walked around the back, she heard the dog whimpering. She looked through the kitchen window and to her horror saw the old gentleman lying on the floor with his dog whimpering next to him. She tried the back door and fortunately it was unlocked. She rushed over to him. She could tell he was still alive. She just stood there panicking, 'Get a grip woman,' she told herself. In her panic, she knelt down and spoke some words of comfort to him;

"Don't worry, you will be fine, I am going to get you some help."

She had no idea if he could hear her. She looked at the sad old dog, wagging his tail and something made fill the dog bowl with water, which the dog heartily drank. She noted a dog flap in the kitchen door so the dog had been able to get in and out. She needed to move quickly, so she dashed out of the bungalow and ran as fast as she could back to the shop. Once inside, Niamh picked up the phone handset and dialled 999. She had no idea how to answer the questions, she was too shocked, she didn't even know the bungalow number but was able to advise the call handler the road name and roughly where the bungalow was situated. She also reassured the operator that she would remain at the bungalow and look out for the emergency services.

She then quickly locked up and ran back to the bungalow and apart from picking up the dog to comfort it, she felt helpless.

Eventually help arrived, the ambulance crew took the elderly gentleman to hospital and the police picked up the dog. She gave her name and address to the police and from the letters on the doormat, the police were able to identify the man's name. He was called Sydney.

Finally, Niamh went back to her flat. She wasn't able to eat much and didn't sleep very well.

Christmas came and Niamh went to her parents home for a few days and a much needed rest. She hadn't finished work until six o'clock on Christmas Eve and her father picked her up from the flat at seven o'clock so it was nearly eight o'clock before they settled down to a Christmas Eve buffet supper. She had a lovely Christmas day and Boxing day with her family before her father dropped her back at the flat the following day.

Niamh went back to work for a few days between Christmas and the New Year. The day before New Year's Eve, a middle aged man came into the shop.

"Sorry to bother you but I have been told by the police that it was a lady who works in this shop who alerted the emergency services about my Uncle Sydney, was that you?"

"Yes, I didn't know your Uncle, it was just that I hadn't seen him walking past for several days, so I went to check on him."

"Oh I'm so glad I have met you. If it wasn't for you he could have died. It seems he had a fall and had been on the floor for several days. The police managed to track me down. I live in Yorkshire and I am very ashamed to say I have neglected coming to see him because I have been so busy with my business... although I am sorry to say, that is not an excuse."

Niamh smiled at him. It was not easy to keep an eye on someone when you live so far away.

He carried on:

"Anyway, I have spent Christmas here, well it wasn't exactly Christmas as we know it, but my uncle is fine and home now, he was severely dehydrated and bruised. He had neglected himself since his wife died, but whilst he was in hospital I cleaned the place up, and have arranged for a cleaner to come in regularly. I've sorted out an alarm to wear around his neck. I have also fitted a key safe around the back of the bungalow. Because the bungalow is detached, the neighbour who lives to the right of him, hadn't noticed anything wrong, but she was very nice and said she would pop round every day from now on. In fact, it's her friend who will clean for him. His beloved dog has also been returned to him. We are so grateful to you and may I ask if you have time, could you pop round? He would be delighted to see you and thank you. From now on I will be down to see him at least once a month and I will also arrange for the repairs on the windows to be done too."

Niamh found time to call round and was pleased to see Sydney, looking so well. She popped in to see him every few days after that and he was making such good progress. By the middle of January, he was back walking with his dog to the shops. Now that he knew Niamh, he waved as he walked by and smiled. She thought he looked so much better but what a shame it took a fall for him to improve.

One day at work Niamh had a great idea. She called at Sydney's on the way home and made him a cup of tea.

"Sydney, how do you feel about coming with me to a pantomime next Sunday?"

Sydney smiled…"That would be brilliant my dear."

On the day of the pantomime, Niamh walked around to Sydney's bungalow. She had arranged a taxi to take them both to the venue. The neighbour was waiting for her and would look after the dog whilst they were out. Sydney was dressed in a shirt and tie, with a smart suit on. He even had a handkerchief pointing out of his top pocket. Niamh realised that Sydney didn't even look like he was stooping over so much, in fact he just looked so smart.

When they arrived at the pantomime venue, Niamh linked her arm through Sydney's and they proudly took their front row seats ready to spot little Aaron!

When the little star began singing, Niamh glanced at Sydney and smiled at the beautiful twinkle in his eye...

Nice memories of the music shop and Paul.

Going the Extra Mile

—ɯ—

"Are you coming for a break, Val?" Carol asked. Val looked at her watch.

"Yes, I will just let Dave know we are both going, it is our allocated time but I'll let him know anyway." Val nipped behind the delicatessen counter where Provisions Manager Dave was filling the fridges with supplies. He winked at Val and smiled when Val told him they were off for a break. The two ladies went off through the staff exit and up the stairs where the staff restaurant was situated. Dave was a great manager, he worked hard, had a cheeky smile and teased his staff in a fun way, but not in an offensive way. The small team, under his leadership, respected him and worked hard to ensure the chilled and frozen food areas of the supermarket always looked fresh and full.

It was the summer of 1984. The upmarket supermarket was very busy particularly on Fridays and Saturdays. Supermarkets didn't open on Sunday's in the 80's. This particular one shut at four o'clock on Saturday afternoons, fairly early compared with other large supermarket chains. Val was due to take a week's holiday beginning the following week. She excitedly told

Carol her plans for the week whilst they sipped their tea during their fifteen minute break. Val was going to Torquay with her husband Paul and his brother and wife. She always had a happy demeanour about her. She came into work with a smile on her face and that's where it stayed during her shifts. A devoted family lady who worshipped her children and their families and never had a bad word to say about anyone. Dave, who was in his fifties, had worked at the supermarket as a Section Manager for many years and Val, also in her fifties, worked part time and started at the supermarket around the same time as Dave. Dave thought highly of Val because she was such a reliable, cheerful person and over the years as trading changed he and Val always had the same work ethic. Carol was younger. She had only worked at the supermarket for a couple of years, worked full time and was equally well thought of by Dave for her conscientious working.

Val went back to her work station after the break and began pricing the packs of butter with the pricing gun. Dave rushed past her a couple of times carrying boxes, whistling as he worked. When Val finished her shift a few hours later, Dave wished her a great holiday.

Just over a week later Val returned from her holiday. Dave enquired if she had had a good time but Val unusually didn't say much about it. She did explain to Dave that it was the first time they had been to Torquay. They had all loved it there and would definitely go back sometime. Dave noticed on that first day back that even though Val had clearly enjoyed the holiday, she was just not her usual self. Dave cracked a few jokes during the course of the day and Val laughed but not in her usual jolly way. Dave was concerned for his friend and work colleague.

Over the week, Dave kept an eye on Val. She continued to work as hard as ever but her sparkle had gone. She still had a smile on her face but a sad look in her eyes. Dave remembered that his section staff were going for a pub meal the following Wednesday, maybe he could chat with Val then? Maybe not, as it might not be the place. Partners were also invited as well. Anyway, for now he would just treat Val in his usual way.

Val didn't work on Saturdays. Dave finished his Saturday shift not long after the shop had shut and returned to his home, a ten minute drive away. It was such a pleasant evening and Dave had bought a selection of meat which he paid for just before the shop shut. On the short journey home, he wondered if his wife Joyce would fancy a barbeque. His meat selection included some sausages and chicken.

"Fancy a barbeque love?" Dave asked Joyce when he walked in through the front door.

"Why not Dave, it's been such a lovely day and we could sit outside. Why don't I phone up our Julie and ask her if they all want to come over? I've got plenty of salad in the fridge."

Two hours later, Dave was donning a crisp white apron and with his pair of tongs was busy flipping the sausages and chicken on their barbeque. Julie, Mitch and their daughter Alice, five, came over. Dave and Joyce's daughter lived nearby and they often had spontaneous gatherings which always turned out such good fun because Dave liked to joke and enjoyed being in the company of others, especially his family.

"How's your week been Julie?" Dave asked.

"It's been good, dad, although Alice's friend has been upset this week, so that upset Alice, but she's okay now. This food is great, what a surprise! I was just looking in the fridge for something quick for tea, then mum rang!"

"What's the matter with Alice's friend, Julie?"

"Not quite sure, dad. Don't like to pry too much but

Alice said she was crying at school, something to do with her family."

Is that the friend we saw her with when we bumped into you all in the town the other day? What was her name?... Oh yes, was it Fay?"

"Yes, dad, nice girl."

Joyce interrupted then, by asking if they all wanted their drinks topping up.

The fun and laughter continued as the balmy summer evening began to turn darker. The solar lights scattered around the garden were gradually lighting up and with all their beautiful colours twinkling in the calm atmosphere, the family felt like they were on holiday.

"Val at work went to Torquay the other week, the English Riviera. She thought it was lovely," Dave said.

"Very nice. Maybe we should look at booking somewhere, Mitch? We haven't been down that way before, we always seem to end up on the East Coast. Could make a nice change and isn't the weather generally better down that way?

"Yes Julie, but in the meantime we better think about getting home! But it's been great, thanks both! Next time it's round ours." Mitch replied.

The happy family evening ended then with Julie, Mitch and Alice setting off for the short walk home.

The weekend soon came to an end and the supermarket was due to open for business again at lunchtime on Monday. This particular chain of supermarkets didn't open on Monday mornings although some staff went in to fill up the shelves and carry out other supermarket tasks. Dave, Val and Carol were all in that morning, ready to restock the provisions section. As they worked hard together getting the supermarket's shelves full and ready for the noon time opening, Dave asked Val how her weekend had been.

"It was fine, thanks Dave," was her short reply.

"It's our get together on Wednesday, Val. Are you bringing Paul?"

"Oh yes, I forgot about that Dave. I don't think we can make it."

Val then, with her trolley walked towards the back door to put the empty cardboard cartons in the baler.

Dave looked at Carol.

"Is Val alright, Carol?"

Carol looked at Dave and frowned.

"I can't really say Dave."

"Why? Has Val told you something in confidence, Carol?"

"She has told me something that is worrying her, not in confidence, but I would feel like I was going behind her back if I talked about it, Dave."

Val then returned with her trolley, free of cartons and carried on working, so nothing more was said.

Wednesday arrived and Dave gathered up the numbers of those coming to the evening's get together.

"Are you sure you and Paul won't be coming tonight Val?" Dave asked.

But Val had not changed her mind. On his break, Dave rang up the Cedars pub and booked ten places, although he was sad that Val and Paul couldn't make it, this was the first time they had missed the regular get togethers.

That evening, Dave and Joyce met up with the other eight. Dave sat next to Carol and all ten of them enjoyed the lovely food and drink and the atmosphere of the old pub.

"Carol, it's such a shame Val and Paul aren't here, can you tell me what is wrong? I've worked with Val for years and she's just not herself. It seemed she had a lovely time in Torquay but what has happened since she came back?"

The others were chatting amongst themselves so no one else heard what Dave said to Carol. Carol decided that she could confide in Dave, knowing he was trustworthy. She also felt the need to unburden. So whilst the others were still talking and laughing she let Dave know that Val came back from her holiday to find a letter from her mother in Australia. Val's parents emigrated to Australia and Val never had got over them leaving. She hadn't ever got on with her father, he was controlling and she felt that her mother would have never had gone halfway around the world if it was her choice. Val didn't understand how they could make a new life without their immediate family. Val's auntie lived out there and they went to live with her. They had rarely travelled back to see Val and her family, and Val and her family had never visited them because it was just too expensive. Val had always felt that her mother was devastated at not being able to spend her time with her and her family. The letter that was on Val's doormat on return from the holiday in Torquay, was to let her know that her father was terminally ill and not expected to live more than another six months. Val was upset because she couldn't afford the flight over, she had little holiday left because she had already used most of it and to make matters worse Paul was likely to be made redundant in the very near future.

"Dave, are you going to the bar to get some drinks?" Joyce piped up and so that was the end of Carol's short conversation with Dave.

Dave jumped up out of his seat.

"Who wants another drink?" He gathered up the glasses and walked off towards the bar. Whilst he was waiting for the drinks, he mulled over what Carol had told him, realising there was little he could do. Maybe she could have some compassionate time off? But how could he arrange that because he wasn't supposed to know?

Over the next few days work carried on as usual. Dave did mention to Val the day after the get together how much they had all missed her and Paul being there. Val smiled at him but didn't pass a comment.

Dave had the weekend off so he finished his late night at eight o'clock after purchasing some food for the weekend making the most of his staff discount. When he got home and was sitting with Joyce at the dinner table eating their spaghetti bolognese, salad and garlic bread, they made some plans of what they would do that weekend. Just as Dave was putting the last of his garlic bread in his mouth, the telephone rang. Joyce, who had finished eating, stood up and went over to the phone situated on the telephone stand with its adjoining padded seat. She picked up the receiver and sat down. It was Julie.

"Hi mum, I've just realised it's dad's weekend off. Do you both fancy going to Wicksteed Park? We are taking a picnic and Alice's friend Fay is going to come. We can take extra for you and dad."

"Sounds great love, let me just check with your dad."

The very next day, Dave and Joyce set off to Wicksteed Park having arranged to meet Julie, Mitch, Alice and Fay at midday.

Once they arrived, they set a blanket on the grass and put some fold up chairs up and enjoyed a large picnic. The two little girls giggled together and both ate well. Mitch had bought a ball and he and the girls began throwing the ball between them. Dave, Joyce and Julie sat on their chairs and chatted in the warm sunshine.

"How is Fay now, Julie?" Joyce asked.

Dave was smiling at the girls running around.

"She has been fine this week. I saw her mum of course, to arrange today. Mind you I don't really know Nicky that well, only because the girls had become such good friends since they started school. She was more than happy for Fay to come with us today. Nicky did mention that she had been crying talking to her mum on the phone because of a family problem and Fay, who she thought was watching the television had seen her mum crying and that had upset her. Nicky said she was upset because her mum's father was in Australia and had been given a terminal diagnosis. She had hoped to have dried her eyes before Fay saw her but she had just walked into the hall where she was."

Dave, who was enjoying watching the girls play, heard the end of the conversation and thought how strange it was that Val had a father in Australia with a terminal illness and also Fay had a great grandad in Australia with a terminal illness. His thoughts were interrupted by Alice pulling his arm.

"Grandad, can we go on the boat over there?"

Dave looked at the large boat on the water.

"Yes, why not," he said, smiling at his granddaughter. "Let's go and get some tickets."

With that, they packed up the blanket, folded up the chairs, gathered up the litter and remains of the picnic and headed back to their cars to offload.

They had a fabulous fun-filled afternoon and set off back to their cars around four o'clock with two tired little girls!

Dave and Joyce felt exhausted on the drive home, so decided to pick up some fish and chips for their tea. They had a quiet evening, enjoying the food and watching a couple of programmes on TV. Later that night when the couple got into bed, Dave thought about Val and Fay. What a coincidence that Australia was talked about twice this week but unfortunately with harrowing circumstances. He was thinking about Val. He obviously knew Paul and that they had two children and two young grandchildren. Because they were always busy at work and he was a man and could never remember his staff's extended family names, he had no idea what Val's family members' names were called. She might have mentioned them, but he hadn't taken any notice. Was it just a coincidence or were they related? He couldn't think they were, Val lived a good twenty minutes drive from where he and Joyce lived. He just assumed Val's family lived close to her. But did they? He didn't really know. Could Fay be Val's granddaughter? Julie didn't know Fay's mum Nicky very well, so she wouldn't know. Dave then shut his eyes and drifted off into a peaceful sleep.

The next morning, Joyce was busy cooking and Dave pottered around the garden. He came in for some coffee about eleven o'clock. They both sat down at the dinner table. Dave decided to tell Joyce his thoughts about Val and Fay. Joyce was already aware of Val's problems because Dave had updated her in the car on the way home from the work get together the previous Wednesday. Joyce listened whilst sipping her steaming coffee.

"You could have a point Dave, but even if Fay is Val's granddaughter, there is nothing we could do to help. I wish we could." It went quiet for a few minutes then Joyce carried on.

"Why don't you call our Julie and tell her what you have told me."

"Okay Joyce, I'll do it now."

He went to the telephone seat. He picked up the receiver and dialled Julie's number. He spoke for a while with Julie, then returned to Joyce who had gone back to making her fruit crumble.

"Joyce, Julie is convinced Val could be Fay's grandma because although Nicky hadn't mentioned her mum's name, she knew they lived in the area where Val and Paul live."

"So, okay then Dave, if we establish they are related, how do we help them? Val clearly needs to go to Australia as soon as possible and there is nothing we can do to help get her there. Anyway Julie is popping round later this afternoon to pick up some cooked chicken for their tea. There's plenty, it's a big chicken you bought and we will still have enough for tomorrow's tea, even after they have taken enough for the three of them."

Julie came round later on. She sat at the table and had a quick cup of coffee with Dave and Joyce.

"Dad, can't you ask at work for Val to have some compassionate leave and some money?" Julie looked at Dave but Joyce answered.

"Do you think we should get involved? After all Val has never told us, only Carol, and we don't want her to be blamed for gossiping." Joyce wasn't trying to dampen their enthusiasm, she was a hundred percent supportive of them, but just trying to look at it from all sides.

"Yes, I get what you are saying, Joyce," Dave replied. "But, I've known Val for years, she's a great work colleague and I don't like seeing her upset, although she tries hard to hide it."

"I agree with dad, mum. Look at what happened with Fay, seeing her mum so upset when talking to her mother."

Joyce smiled at them both. 'They will do what they have to do,' she thought.

"When I go into work, I will have a private word with Steve," Dave said to them both. Steve was the store manager.

On Thursday of the following week, Steve called Dave into his office. Dave had spoken with Steve at the beginning of the week.

"Dave, I have spoken with the head office and they have agreed Val can have compassionate leave and they have also agreed to contribute half of the airfare from a fund set aside to help staff in need."

"That's great, Steve. Thanks a lot, I will try and work out how we can raise some more, then we have to work out how to talk to Val about it and whether she will accept the money. The last thing we want to do is cause any offence."

That evening Dave rang Julie.

"Thing is dad, how are we going to raise the rest of the money? It's great that you have got what you have from work…Just had a thought, how about we do a car boot a week on Sunday? The one on the field off Mill Street is on every Sunday. I can ask Mitch's family to sort out unwanted stuff and I have lots of bits here."

"Good idea Julie, I will see what I can rustle up too, but we will still need to think of something else to raise the rest."

Car boot sales had been happening for several years and were getting very popular in the 80's with crowds of people looking for bargains.

Dave was quite touched by Julie's enthusiasm to help Val. He admired her willingness to help but didn't want to disappoint her and say that the small amount of money they could make on their unwanted items would be just a drop in the ocean to what was needed to make up the shortfall.

"Bless her," he said to Joyce who was sitting on the sofa flicking through the TV Times to look at what was on the television that evening. He went to sit next to her. "She's a great kid, our Julie."

Joyce smiled at him.

"She always was considerate, even when she was a little girl." she replied.

The following week, Steve caught up with Dave. Dave updated Steve that he and Julie were doing a car boot sale to try and raise a bit more money.

"You know what Dave, we have lots of stuff I could sell. My garage is full of items from when we helped clear out my parent's home after they downsized. It needs getting rid of. Maybe we could do it too? I'm happy to give any money we make to you to add to the total. I'll check with Sally when I get home, it could be fun and I know Sally would like the garage cleared out so we can put the car in again!"

Dave felt quite pleased after the conversation with Steve. He noticed that Val's eyes were sad, but she was still smiling and being her usual kind self. He just hoped that they could help her without her feeling that they had poked their noses into her business.

One afternoon when Val had gone home, Dave felt he needed to update Carol. He asked Carol if she could just stay for a couple of minutes after work. She agreed and Dave put her in the picture.

"You know what Dave, I think I will come to the car boot and sell some items I want to get rid of. I can sort it all out on Saturday."

Dave was smiling to himself as he drove home. It was now turning into a work car boot event! It was great though, how the others were all rallying around to help.

Sunday came around and Dave and Julie arrived at the field at seven o'clock, an early start to make sure they got a good spot. As soon as Dave opened his boot to pull his paste table out, people were crowding around to see what was inside. By the time he had set up the table, Julie had sold many items just from the boot and was thoroughly enjoying herself. They never stopped for the next hour, with many items being sold before the table display was completed.

By nine o'clock, Julie was able to manage so Dave walked around and found Carol busy selling. He called her name and waved as he walked by, not wanting to interrupt her sales. He then found Steve and Sally who were also busy. He picked up two teas from the hot food van. He was cheerfully walking back to Julie carrying the drinks, when he felt a tap on his back. He turned around and nearly spilled the tea…it was Val and Paul!

'Keep calm' he thought. 'Val has no idea why we are all here.'

"Hi Dave," Val said. "I've just seen Carol and Steve, aren't they paying you all enough at the supermarket?!!" she laughed. Dave laughed too.

"Looks that way doesn't it! How are you Paul?"

The three of them chatted for a few minutes. Val said to Dave that they were just looking for some cheap cleaning items. They were trying to save some money because Paul could lose his job any day. It was the first time Val had indicated any problems to Dave. Dave then made his excuses and took Julie the much needed drink.

At the end of a long morning Dave and Julie returned to Dave's home where Mitch and Alice were waiting for them along with Joyce who had prepared an appetising buffet and had set it out on the table. After they had all eaten, Mitch and Julie sat and counted up the money. Dave, Joyce and Alice went into the kitchen to tidy up. Afterwards, Dave took a tray of coffees and a squash for Alice into the lounge.

Julie looked excited and let everyone know the grand total of their sales from their hard work. Dave was amazed just how much there was. It had far exceeded his expectations, especially as it was just from their unwanted items. He knew that they needed far more to be able to support Val but he was pleasantly pleased.

On Monday morning when the shop was shut ready to open at noon, Steve invited Carol and Dave to his office.

"Great morning wasn't it both?" he said to them. "Did you both do well?"

Carol and Dave reported to Steve how much money they had raised. Steve congratulated them both.

"That's brilliant! I also have some great news. As you know we were mainly selling my parents unwanted things. There was a piece of china that a dealer spotted and he offered me more than what we could ever imagine. He said it was part of one of his collections and it was one thing that was missing. When we got home I felt it was only fair to offer the money to my parents even though we had their blessings to sell theirs stuff. My parents didn't want a penny."

When Steve told Carol and Dave the amount he and Sally had made they were both speechless. With the three totals added to the contribution from the supermarket, there was more than enough to get Val to Australia and back so the sooner they spoke with Val about it the better.

Dave went home that evening and as soon as he had eaten, went over to the telephone table, sat down and dialled Julie's number. As he waited for her to answer he fiddled about with the coiled phone wire attached from the handset to the phone base. It didn't matter how much you tried to keep the coiled wire on these phones from getting twisted, they somehow still did. Julie finally answered.

"We're so proud of you Julie."

Dave then went on to relay the story to her. Julie was thrilled and just hoped their efforts would help Val. Next, Dave phoned Steve to discuss how they were going to give the money to Val.

The very next day when the store was quieter around late morning Steve called Val over the tannoy to go to his office. Val was a bit shocked and immediately rushed off the shop floor and up the stairs to Steve's office. She knocked on the door.

"Is everything okay Mr King?" she asked Steve.

Steve asked her to take a seat where he relayed the whole story. Val was totally overwhelmed. Steve passed her a tissue. She just couldn't take in what her work colleagues had done for her and how, when she saw them at the car boot sale that they were all doing it for her.

"Val, I'm going to get Carol and Dave."

He left Val for a few minutes and got a message put out on the tannoy for them both to come to the office. When they arrived Val hugged them both. There were tears all round but then Val managed to speak.

"I will pay you all back, I really will. You do not know how much this means to me."

Dave shook his head.

"No Val, You most definitely won't. We're your friends and we wanted to help. But, there is a bit more to it. My granddaughter Alice is a friend of your granddaughter. Julie, my daughter was the one who suggested the car boot sales when she put two and two together and realised Nicky was your daughter."

Val was stunned, but when she had taken it all in, she said to Dave that Nicky had told her that Fay had a nice friend in Alice and they had been to Wicksteed Park!

"Thinking about it Dave, Fay told me Alice's grandparents went too!"

"Yes, that was Joyce and me. We had a great time, they are fantastic kids."

They all had a few minutes to chat before they resumed back into their professional roles ready for the store to open for its afternoon trade.

Just one week later Val began her compassionate leave and flew off to her parents in Australia. Her father passed away just a week after Val arrived in Australia.

The months passed, Christmas was on its way and the store was beginning to get very busy. Dave had organised the work Christmas meal for his staff and their partners and families, the more, the merrier. He was so pleased that Val and Paul were able to come this time. Paul had lost his job but had soon found another better paid one. Despite the loss of her father Val had returned to work and had gradually returned to her old self.

A week before the meal, Val asked Dave a question.

"Dave, would it be okay if Paul and I bring another one to the meal?"

"Sure Val, have you got a boyfriend as well as Paul?" he joked. He was pleased that he could crack jokes again and have a bit of friendly banter with Val like they used to.

"Don't be daft Dave!" Val laughed and gave him a playful tap on his arm.

She then looked serious.

"No Dave, it's my mum, she's coming home tomorrow. She's here to stay and she's going to live with us. It's where she belongs. We have a lot of lost time to make up for."

Dave felt a lump in his throat and smiled at Val. She smiled back and they both walked up the stairs to the staff restaurant. Dave turned to Val when they reached the top.

"Happy Christmas Val. We can't wait to meet her."

Val grinned at Dave, he was certainly one in a million, prepared to go the extra mile…

Remembering Dave (Centre)

A Provisions Manager

Certainly the nicest, funniest boss I have ever had the pleasure of working with.

Dedicated also to my great friends Val and Paul

The Hidden Years

—w—

THE YEAR WAS 1970. Emma was ten years old and was organising different outfits for her Barbie dolls on the floor in the dining area of the family home in Nottingham.

"Mum, can we watch the fireworks from Grandad's window on bonfire night?" she asked Jeanette, who had just walked in with some cutlery to lay the table for the family tea time.

"I can ask Grandad if he doesn't mind you and Bob using his room for an hour," she replied.

Their four bedroom home was situated in a cul de sac, high up on a hill, on a large housing estate. From one of the front bedrooms which Grandad used, the view from the window looked down on the city of Nottingham.

"I'm glad you are asking him mum, he's scary," Emma replied.

Grandad was a giant in Emma's eyes, well over six foot tall, a man of few words who rarely smiled. He had moved into the family's four bedroom detached home when Emma's Grandma had passed away some seven months earlier. Grandma and Grandad had lived nearby in the city, until they sold their home and moved to Spain to live with Emma's auntie six years earlier.

Janette was slightly perturbed by Emma's comment at her Grandad being scary. He had been a good father to her, although rarely smiled or showed any emotion and didn't speak much. But she hadn't really considered before how his mannerisms made Emma feel scared of him.

Jeanette had never got on with her sister, Liz who had moved to Spain when she married a Spanish waiter she had met when the family had been for a holiday. Jeanette had been fourteen then and Liz three years older. On that holiday the family only saw Liz at mealtimes, she had been too busy mixing with other young people…including the Spanish waiter. When Liz turned eighteen, she booked a flight to Spain and never returned. Jeanette had her doubts that the marriage would last because they never had any money, Carlos didn't earn much money as a waiter and Liz didn't work, she spent her time bringing up their three daughters.

Jeanette didn't like her sister when they were young children, she thought she was a selfish prima donna. In recent times, Liz was regularly asking their parents to send money over to her. Jeanette was livid when Liz managed to persuade their parents to sell their small house and rent a tiny flat in Spain near them. She desperately tried to talk her parents out of selling up but they were so tempted by a relaxing life of sun and the beach. Jeanette assumed that they thought the grass would be greener on the other side and she knew her mum struggled with the cold damp English winters because of her respiratory problems. She was so worried that Liz would have them looking after her children and paying for everything she could possibly get them to pay for.

With Spain only a two hour flight away, her parents did come back to England frequently and stayed with Jeanette and her family mainly in the warmer months but sometimes at Christmastime. After four years, Liz had fleeced them of all their money from the sale of the house and when they were of no use to her, she suggested they go back to England. So, in 1968 Jeanette's parents returned to England and with little money left, moved in with Jeanette, Jim, Bob and Emma. Jim was very tolerant and supportive of the situation and spent a great deal of time trying to find a way of cheaply rehoming the couple, so they could lead some kind of independent life in their later years.

Because of Grandma's respiratory problems, there had to be no stairs so eventually he managed to find a ground floor flat to rent in the city for them. For about eighteen months Grandma and Grandad lived in the flat. They were regular visitors to Jeanette and Jim for Sunday lunch or a weekday tea. Jeanette had nothing more to do with Liz, she was so annoyed by her selfish greed and taking advantage of her parents good nature.

It was a big shock when Grandma died suddenly. She collapsed, went into hospital and two days laters she passed away. It was all so very quick and they were all in a state of shock. Liz didn't even come over for the funeral. Grandad found he could not afford to stay in the flat and wasn't really capable of looking after himself, so he came back to live with Jeanette and family.

It had been a difficult period in their lives and sometimes having Grandad living there restricted what the family could do. He did tend to sit around, making it difficult for any of the family to have their friends around, particularly as he wasn't the most sociable person. If he wasn't sitting around, he could be found at the top of the garden smoking. Jeanette thought it might be an idea to get him to mix with people his own age. She decided she would make some enquiries to see if there were any social clubs for senior citizens nearby.

It was coming up to November 5th and the family including Grandad were preparing to have a bonfire and a few fireworks and sparklers in the garden. Afterwards, Bob and Emma were going to watch the fireworks over Nottingham for an hour before their bedtime.

On the evening of the 5th, Bob and Emma were very excited and before the fireworks they made some toffee in the kitchen whilst Jim nailed the Catherine Wheels onto the fence and stood the rockets into milk bottles, placing them around the edge of the garden. Grandad, with a cigarette hanging out of his mouth, attempted to get the bonfire started. Jeanette was in the kitchen. She wrapped potatoes in foil to bake on the bonfire. She also put some sausages in the oven and sliced baps for hotdogs. It was such a fun evening for the family, especially for the children. Even Grandad smiled at times, something of a rarity.

The fireworks were beautiful, the food was delicious and luckily, the weather stayed fine for the evening.

Afterwards, Bob helped his dad clear up the garden, Grandad went and sat in the lounge to watch TV and Jeanette tidied up in the kitchen. Emma went upstairs into Grandad's room, not somewhere where she normally ventured. She looked around it whilst she waited for Bob. It was quite sparse, with a few clothes folded up on the chair. She saw some items on the bedside table including a book, glasses case and a comb. There was also a folded up piece of paper. As she was getting bored waiting for Bob, she picked up the piece of paper and opened it. She read a few lines, which said…'*Thank you Albert for your kind offer of inviting me to stay with you. I think it would be a good idea because I feel like a nuisance here, not being related…*'

The door banged open and in marched Bob who immediately turned off the lights, whilst Emma quickly threw the paper back to where she found it. They both leant on the window sill watching the amazing firework displays going off all over the city. Eventually, the two children went off to their separate bedrooms to go to bed. Once settled, Emma lay in the dark thinking about the letter. She was secretly pleased Grandad might be leaving although she did not understand what he meant by not being related, but then she knew she shouldn't have read the letter so it was a secret she had to keep forever.

A week later Jeanette had found a club nearby where Grandad could go in the afternoons to spend time with people in his age group. Over the evening meal she brought it up. Grandad looked a bit uncomfortable, so when he finished his mouthful he spoke.

"It's nice of you to find me somewhere to visit, but I have actually made some plans. I don't want to impose anymore on all of you, so my old friend Albert, who lost his wife a few years ago has invited me to lodge at his house."

Emma looked down at her plate. She was glad that it was out that he was leaving, but what about the 'not related' bit?

Grandad stayed with the family until after Christmas then left to live with Albert. It couldn't come soon enough for Emma. She just wished he had laughed and joked like some of her other friends Grandads did. He had made her feel nervous, something she hadn't felt when Grandma was alive, because Grandma was just the best Grandma she could wish for, and Emma hadn't noticed how strange Grandad was then.

The years passed by.

In 2018 Emma was in her late fifties with a family of her own. She was married to Richard and they had two daughters and one granddaughter. Emma was so happy watching Richard joking and smiling when he was playing with their granddaugher, particularly after experiencing her Grandad's sullen face. Grandad had passed away two years after he left to live with Albert. She didn't go to his funeral because in those days, children rarely attended them. She did know that her mum's sister Liz didn't come over for it, infact her mum and Liz never spoke again. As far as she was aware, there was only her parents, Albert and a few friends who attended the funeral.

Jeanette and Jim were still in good health and moved to Sutton-on-Sea, when they retired. Emma and her family were always visiting or they came over to them. Bob had moved up North, married and had two boys.

One day, out of the blue, Emma received a Facebook message. She didn't know who it was from but was able to open it and read it and find out if it was genuine or spam. It read:

Hi Emma, You don't know me but I am your cousin Rosa. My mum and your mum were sisters. Sadly my mum and dad are both dead but I have always known a family secret and if you are happy to talk to me I will tell you. I'm sorry we have missed out on being cousins and seeing each other whilst we were growing up, but now my sisters and I have no other family, we wanted to connect with you and Bob and maybe with your mum? You are our only family and it's not our fault that our parents fell out.

Emma sat down on the chair and thought about the message. It was quite true that none of them were involved in their parents' fall out. She decided that she would write back to Rosa but not mention it to her mother yet.

The pair exchanged messages for a couple of weeks, just

catching up on each other's families and their lives. One day Emma received a message that shocked her.

Hi Emma, now we have caught up, there is something I have kept to myself since I was a child but feel it is time to confide in you. As you know I was the eldest child and one day when Grandma and Grandad were at ours, I heard them having an argument. My sisters were in the yard playing, dad was working and mum was in the kitchen. When I heard them arguing I listened. I know I shouldn't have but I couldn't help it. Grandad said to Grandma that the problems between the daughters were not his problem, because they were not his. He couldn't help it if he wasn't able to father children and she had to go and find other men to give them a family life. Grandma then began crying and told him that his comments were so unfair because he had agreed never to mention what happened and bring their daughters up as his own. He was the one who encouraged her to find other men so they could have the family they so desperately wanted. I have never mentioned this to anyone Emma, but if our mum's had different fathers, maybe it had something to do with how different they were.

Emma was dumbstruck when she read the message. Memories came flooding back of the time she had read the letter in Grandad's bedroom. Both girls had looked and listened to things they shouldn't have and had to carry the burden of their findings to themselves until this point.

Emma replied to Rosa explaining about the letter she read in Grandad's room all those years ago. They both agreed to think about each other's confessions and talk again the next day.

The next day Rosa sent a message to Emma. She told Emma that she had been putting together a family tree on a website and they also sold DNA kits and what did Emma think about them doing DNA tests? Emma was shocked when she read the message because she too had herself just started doing the same thing and had noticed DNA kits for sale but had never thought there was ever a need to do one. They both decided that was the way forward.

Emma decided that she would not mention any of this to her parents. Richard was very supportive of what they were doing. Emma had relayed the whole story about the letter and she had felt it such a relief to unburden to both Rosa and Richard after all this time. Emma had no idea if her mother had any clue that the man she called father may not have been her blood father. She decided that she would tell Bob. Bob was very understanding as she expected him to be, he did surprise Emma by deciding that he too would do the DNA test.

The test kits arrived and each of the three completed their tests and eventually the test results arrived. It was clear that Bob and Emma were obviously brother and sister. Emma suspected that Bob just did his DNA test out of curiosity and to support her, there was never any doubt that they were brother and sister!

What the tests did reveal was that Bob and Emma only shared one grandparent with Rosa. This confirmed what they had begun to suspect, that Grandad was not their blood Grandad. What happened further was something none of them had even thought about. Rosa had a strong connection with another lady on the website and Emma and Bob had a strong connection with a man. Between them they decided to send a message to these people and see if they could find how they may be related. Over the weeks, messages went to and fro between various people and eventually they managed to piece together what they had discovered.

Emma and Bob had still decided not to mention this to their parents yet. Both Jeanette and Jim were still young at heart, active people who they knew would be able to accept what they had done, but they felt they wanted to complete the story as much as they could.

Finally, they had all discovered from the power of DNA, who their Grandad's were. Rosa had been in contact with a lady Miriam, who was in her seventies and lived in Nottingham. She was aware that her father had another child with a married lady and she explained the story to Rosa. He hadn't known the lady was married until after they had consummated their relationship. He found out from a friend and he went round to her home where he had originally thought she lived with her parents. He went during the day in the hope that her husband was at work, to have it out with her. She brutally explained that she wanted a baby but her husband was unable to make her pregnant. She told him to go away and leave them to bring up the baby. He was very upset, so he moved to another area of Nottingham, met Miriam's mother and they had Miriam and her sister. It was never a secret but there was nothing the family could do about it.

Grandma must have wanted another baby to complete the family. Between them, Bob, Emma and Rosa had worked out that this was all planned with Grandad's consent. What Emma and Bob found out from their investigations was that they had possibly connected with the half brother of their mum Jeanette! Keith lived alone, he was divorced but had no children. He had been doing a family tree of his relatives mainly out of interest and for something to do in retirement. Keith's mother had died during childbirth and he was brought up by his father. He recalled when he was about seven his father had a lady friend around sometimes and she had a young child with her, but it wasn't for long and then his father met another lady and married. Keith agreed that there was every possibility that his father could also be Jeanette's father, Emma and Bob's blood grandfather. Keith suggested that he and Jeanette also do DNA tests and confirm it. This meant that Emma had to break quite a bit of news to her parents. It also turned out that Keith only lived a couple of streets away from where Jeanette and Jim used to live. To think that for many years, Emma's mum had a half brother living close by!

Emma was beginning to wish she had confided in her parents when Rosa first made contact because so much had happened, but so much more than they could have ever envisaged. She wondered what had put her off telling her mother right from the start but then she concluded it was a couple of things, one being her looking at Grandad's private letter when she was a kid and then the fact that her mum and Liz never spoke and she knows her mum would not even be aware that Liz had died. 'Goodness' she thought. 'This is such a lot to take in.'

Emma and Richard were due to visit Sutton-on-Sea and spend a few days with her parents so Emma figured this would have to be the time to explain the whole story. She kept in touch with Keith and would let him know if Jeanette decided to take the DNA test.

Whilst Richard drove to Sutton-on-Sea one Friday evening after work, Emma quietly sat in the passenger seat, thinking about the whole situation. If it was confirmed Keith was her mum's brother, what a shame they had all those wasted years. Keith was now in his late eighties and although he said on the phone he kept himself fit and well, she couldn't help but dwell on the fact that he would have made a lovely extra family member. Keith told Emma that he had an active and full life including many activities to keep himself fit, including golf. He was also 'not bad' when using the computer!

Jeanette had made a lovely buffet for when the couple arrived. The four of them sat in the lounge with the plates of delicious food on their knees. Emma updated Jeanette on how the family were all getting on. Jim took the empty plates out to the kitchen when they had all finished and came back with a tray of teas.

Emma then took the plunge and began the whole story. Jeanette smiled and although surprised by it all was not totally shocked. Jeanette was a practical, pleasant lady who took everything in her stride.

"Wow, I knew absolutely nothing about any of this, however I don't know why but I suspected that dad may not be my blood father. For no other reason than it was just something that I thought. He was a good father but always held back a bit with decisions mum had to make for us girls, like it wasn't anything to do with him. Strange really. I think I just noticed he didn't behave like my friends' dads did. I don't blame them for what they did, mum was a lovely devoted mother and generally they were happy together. It does upset me though that they didn't consider the consequences in other people's lives, particularly Rosa's grandfather who knew that he had another child and had to live his life not knowing her."

She was sitting next to Emma and put her arm around her shoulder.

"You should have told me about the letter, instead of keeping it to yourself. You were only a child, children do things like that."

Emma smiled, whilst Jeanette carried on.

"Anyway, I'm happy to do the DNA test, I quite like the idea of having a brother even at my age! Liz and I just never got on and the final straw was when she made Grandma and Grandad sell their home. It would be great for us all to meet up with Rosa, her sisters and their families. The fall out between me and Liz had nothing to do with them."

The four of them carried on chatting until late into the evening and Emma agreed she would order the DNA kit for her mum.

A few months later, the DNA result came back and confirmed that Jeanette and Keith were half siblings. There was a plan for Emma, Richard and her parents to take a trip to Spain to meet Rosa, her sisters and their families. It was exciting for Emma to have some extended family. Rosa hoped to meet up with her mum's half sisters in England, but whether it would happen or not remained to be seen.

Emma phoned Keith to confirm what they already knew. He was such a charming man on the phone, she couldn't wait to meet him. They arranged to meet in a restaurant in Nottingham when her parents were coming to stay.

The time came for Emma, Richard, Jeanette and Jim to meet up with Keith. Emma had booked a table for them at a restaurant very close to where Keith lived and where Jeanette and Jim had lived. Jeanette and Jim arrived at Emma's on a Friday evening. The meal was booked for the Saturday evening, which left the daytime on Saturday for them to spend time with Emma's family. Eventually, Richard drove them to the restaurant. They all walked inside and headed to the bar.

Emma looked around the busy bar area looking for an older man sitting on his own, who would be Keith but she needn't have bothered.

"Hi, Keith, long time no see!" Jeanette said to Keith who was sitting at the bar. Keith stood up from the bar stool and could not believe his eyes. "Jeany..."

Emma looked at Richard, they were both wondering what was going on…so was Jim!

Keith laughed. "Well fancy you Jeany, being my kid sister!"

'What is going on?' Emma thought.'Jeany? I've never known my mum being called that.'

Jeanette laughed, "I think we better put them out of their misery Keith. I never thought for one minute it was you. When we worked at the hospital, you were just Keith, the porter."

When Jeantte's children went to high school, she took a part time clerical job at the city hospital. Keith was a porter and often used to come into the ward and tease Jeanette. He used to say she had a 'posh' name and that's why he shortened it to Jeany. It was all in fun. Keith had loved his job, he was a sociable man. It was quite something to be sitting in a restaurant with a lady he worked alongside for nearly twenty years…who unbeknown to both of them at the time…was his sister!

Emma felt tears in her eyes. This was such a wonderful moment and then it dawned on her, this whole happy day was brought about by Rosa and herself…being nosey kids!

This was most definitely a secret that Grandma and 'Grandad' couldn't take to their graves…because of the amazing science of Deoxyribonucleic Acid better known as DNA.

For the Love of our Furry Friends

—∿—

"Put the paper down Rupert," Celia demanded. Rupert raised an eyebrow, folded up the paper and looked at her.

"Celia, you have my complete attention."

He knew what was coming, because recently when Chloe was not around, Celia brought up the subject.

"You don't seem to realise the importance, Rupert," she looked at him crossly.

"Yes, I do but we can't run our children's lives. Chloe is just laid back, she will sort out what she wants to achieve in her life, just give her time."

"Yes, too laid back, a bit like you." Celia walked off into the kitchen, sighing.

Chloe was seventeen and in her final year at school, with no indication of what she wanted to do when she finished after her 'A' levels the following spring. Jack, just a year older, had taken a gap year to travel and would return ready to go to Bristol University the following September. Over the past three months or so, Celia and Rupert had been coming to blows in their discussions over Chloe's future. Celia was becoming more uptight about it but Rupert was happy if Chloe was happy, and Chloe was a happy young lady.

Rupert was a dentist, a partner in a busy practice in the city. Celia had her own Podiatry practice. She wanted the best for her children and expected them to both go into 'professional roles'. Rupert, on the other hand, was more easy going and of course he wanted them to do well, but more importantly, they were content and happy in whatever route they chose.

Celia walked back into the dining room.

"You are so frustrating Rupert. Look at my friend Stella, both her children have gone to university and are doing so well, with great job opportunities ahead. Her girls have lovely haircuts and look so tidy, whereas our Chloe dyes her hair weird colours, not to mention it's far too long, full of split ends."

It was Rupert's turn to sigh.

"For goodness sake Celia, you are comparing our daughter with your friends. That's very unfair. Chloe is a lovely, caring girl. I'm very proud of her. I'm proud of both our kids. Just give it a rest for now."

"I'm sorry Rupert, blue hair, it's not funny. Stella must wonder what we have done wrong."

With that Rupert ran his hand through his hair, stood up and spoke quietly.

"What does it matter what Stella thinks? That's a ridiculous thing to say."

The days passed by in a similar way. One day Rupert was outside trimming the overgrown foliage. Chloe came out to him and they chatted and laughed. They had a good relationship so Rupert decided he would gently broach the hair subject. His life was getting difficult with Celia and he wanted to do something to please her, even if he didn't quite agree with her.

"Chloe, your mum would like you to have your hair trimmed. I know it's your hair but just to keep the peace… Just an inch or two…please?… Pretty please!" he joked.

Chloe glared at him, then she burst out laughing.

"I know mum hates my hair and sometimes I just colour it with a bright colour to annoy her! Sorry dad! Yes of course I will. Mind you, if it's just to make your life easier, you can pay for me to go to a nice, modern, expensive salon!! Is that a deal dad?"

Rupert laughed too.

"For a peaceful life, a big yes!"

They were both chuckling away, when Celia came out to them.

"What are you two finding so funny?"

"Just told dad a joke, mum."

That satisfied Celia so the three of them went inside and had lunch together.

One week later, Chloe set off into town for her hair appointment at one of the top salons in the area. She hadn't told her mum or dad, but she was fed up with her long hair and had decided to get it all chopped off and have a modern short style. She wasn't going to let them have it all their way though, she had booked to have another vibrant colour put on, a bright orange shade.

She arrived at the salon about fifteen minutes early and sat down on a comfy chair to wait. There were no magazines to read anymore in places like the salon, because there had been a pandemic and all unnecessary items that may spread germs were removed. Chloe removed her phone from her pocket. She looked at her Facebook and flicked through her profile pictures.

There were some with all her different hair colours on her long flowing locks, which were about to be cut off. She suddenly panicked and wondered if she would like her hair short. Yes, she decided, it was time for a change and if she didn't like it, it would grow back. She smiled to herself and thought of her mum. Her mum would love the short hair but not the colour, but hey ho, she might look neater than her mum's snobby friend's daughter. 'Miss perfect Lucinda,' she thought, and then frowned. 'No that mustn't happen, I don't want to look too neat, that's not my style.'

Chloe scrolled down her news feed, then suddenly she stopped because an item that one of her friends had shared caught her eye. She read with great interest. There was a story about a Beagle breeding farm where the animals were used for testing. She was pleased to read that a group of people had set up a camp and had regular demonstrations. Petitions had also been set up to highlight the horrors. She was still reading when her name was called. She quickly closed the window and put her phone back into her pocket. She explained to the hairdresser exactly what she wanted done and throughout the long process, she just thought about what she had read.

Some three hours later, a hot and happy Chloe left the salon. She loved her new look, although it was strange not having long hair. She walked into home and Celia did a double take.

"I can't believe it's you!"

"Yes, it's me mum. Do you like the colour?" Chloe asked, expecting a negative response.

"I love it all Chloe, it's fabulous." Celia put her arm around Chloe and gave her a kiss on her cheek. Chloe resisted asking her if she looked better than Lucinda.

Chloe's mind kept going back to the camp which was set up outside the breeding farm. There was something in what she read where she felt she needed to go to the camp to visit. She looked up where it was and also if there was a bus to get there and back so she could go for the day. She decided to bring it up at teatime, because again she knew her mum wouldn't approve, so she might as well face the music and get it out the way.

As expected, her mum was unhappy about her going, but as usual Rupert could understand Chloe's reasons for wanting to go. Chloe loved dogs, she loved all animals but just couldn't resist dogs. The family had never been able to have a dog because Jack suffered with a lot of allergies including an allergy to pet hair. In the past, they had rabbits outside in the garage but that was all.

Chloe managed to make her way to the camp and back. Celia and Rupert noticed a change in their bubbly, unpredictable daughter after that day. On return, Chloe declared herself a vegetarian and she wanted to prepare her own meals. Celia was not impressed even though they were not great meat eaters, preferring fish, however, Rupert supported Chloe. He suggested when she cooks for herself, she could sometimes include a portion for him.

One day, over the teatime meal, where Chloe was enjoying a mediterranean vegetable lasagne, she announced something to her parents;

"I've got a voluntary job, dog walking at the rescue centre."

The rescue centre was a couple of miles away in the countryside.

"Well done Chloe."

Rupert looked at her as he munched his meat lasagne, although he did think Chloe's looked more appetising.

Celia wasn't so impressed, but decided not to pass negative comments. She couldn't understand where the compassion for dogs came from. Rupert and herself were not particularly interested in pets. They didn't dislike pets, they just didn't fit into their lives.

Chloe loved the job. She adored all the dogs and spent a lot of time at the centre going there after school and Saturday mornings.

She chatted all through mealtimes to Celia and Rupert about each dog she walked and their different personalities. Rupert just loved her enthusiasm. Celia tried to be interested but couldn't understand why Chloe would prefer to work with dogs than people, like her and Rupert.

The exams were looming for Chloe. She wasn't interested in revising, she was too busy with the dogs. April came and Chloe was so popular at the rescue centre, she was asked if she would like a full time job there. Chloe was over the moon. It was her dream job and she was told she could start as soon as her exams were over. The little interest she had shown in exams waned even more. She couldn't wait to get them over and the minute she had finished school was the time she began the job.

Chloe muddled her way through the exams, not really caring what the outcome may be. She felt her life vocation had come, the minute she began the job. A job which she never considered to be work. When she received her first payslip at the end of the month, she actually couldn't believe she was paid for doing something she loved. She was extremely popular with both the other staff members and volunteers. One day, she suggested to the manager that they have a Fun Day to raise funds to help keep the centre going. Something that hadn't been done before, so the manager asked Chloe if she would like to arrange it.

Chloe threw herself into the role which was to be held on the first Saturday in September. She organised various traders to pay for stalls to sell their goods, she organised for people to loan them gazebos, she arranged people to make cakes and provide refreshments and she begged local businesses to help out by donating money, goods or anything that would help on the day. She spent her evenings putting up posters to advertise the event and even chatted on the local radio when the event was just three days away.

Rupert was extremely impressed by her dedication and hard work. Celia was finding it all alot to take in. It was the last place she expected her daughter to work at. Her vision was that her daughter would follow in the family footsteps and would have expected Chloe to graduate with a degree in a subject such as Speech and Language Therapy, or any other profession within the health and social care spectrum.

At teatime on the Thursday before the big Fun Day, Chloe looked at her mum and dad.

"What time are you both coming on Saturday? I might be too busy to talk to you but look out for me!"

Celia looked horrified. Did Chloe really expect her to walk around a field and admire the dogs in their pens? Rupert and her never spent their Saturdays doing that, they went to the local shopping centre and generally had coffee and a cake whilst they were there.

Rupert was first to speak.

"Of course we will look out for you Chloe, we'll look forward to it! Say around eleven?"

Celia glared at him.

"Oh, oh, yes, Chloe, that's fine." Celia put her head down and put a fork into her sausage which she had purchased from the local farm shop. She suddenly lost the will to eat it. She was getting increasingly uncomfortable eating meat, with Chloe dead set against it.

Rupert heaved a sigh of relief. At least she said the right thing. He figured that if they went there in the morning, they could then go on to the shopping centre for cake and coffee. It's a hard life keeping the peace, he smiled to himself.

Saturday arrived. Rupert and Celia hadn't even heard Chloe leave the house. They woke up at seven thirty, so had no idea what time Chloe had got up.

They both did the normal Saturday morning jobs, after they had eaten breakfast. They were just about to leave to set off for Fun Day, when Rupert noticed Celia's footwear.

"We are walking around a field as well as hard standing, Celia. Don't you think you might need some more substantial footwear.

"Rupert, I am a foot specialist, I'm not used to being told what to wear on my feet."

As she was speaking, she looked down and although she didn't want to admit it, he was probably right. She didn't like the thought of going to the shopping centre in her clean white trainers after though. Eventually, she put her trainers on and put her neat sandals in a bag for later. Rupert was still not convinced the immaculate trainers were suitable still, but they were the best out of a bad job.

Rupert drove his Jaguar car over the bumpy makeshift car park in a field across the road from the rescue centre. They walked from the car on the grass, avoiding the masses of rabbit droppings and crossed the road to the centre. They paid the entrance fee and began to join the crowds milling around. Rupert felt incredibly proud that his daughter had organised this massive event. Celia was looking down at her trainers, realising she hadn't avoided all the rabbit droppings.

They began by looking along the pens which contained each rescue dog.

"Oh look, Rupert, there's Millie, who Chloe talks about a lot. Isn't she gorgeous?"

Rupert looked shocked. Did that really come out of his wife's mouth?

Things just got better, Celia admired all the dogs, splashed out on raffle tickets, chatted with staff and also informed them all she was Chloe's mother. Rupert was overjoyed. During this time, there was no sign of Chloe. They made their way to the field which was full of gazebos and brimming with people. They still couldn't see Chloe, but they carried on walking around each gazebo, buying craft items (which they probably didn't need) and generally supporting the day. Celia saw children queuing up at one gazebo and looked inside. To her surprise, she saw Chloe sitting with a child. Chloe had nearly finished face painting a little girl. The beautiful design she had painted on her face was amazing.

Chloe looked up, saw them and grinned.

"We didn't know you could face paint? But it looks great Chloe." Celia said as Chloe had just finished painting. The little girl was admiring herself in the mirror, whilst her mother paid Chloe.

"She's done a marvellous job then!" the mother of the child said to Celia. "You obviously have a very talented daughter."

Celia beamed at the lady.

"I have a wonderful daughter, thank you."

Chloe stood up and had a quick chat with her parents.

"The other face painter didn't show up to help Sam, so I just stood in over a busy spell. Are you two off shopping now?"

Rupert looked at Celia expecting her to say, yes.

"No, we have had such a lovely day so far, I don't want it to end, so we will have coffee and cake here Chloe. We can add a bit more money to the fund."

Rupert winked at Chloe.

Later, that evening a tired but elated Chloe returned home. To her surprise, Celia had made a big vegetable risotto for the three of them. Chloe was thrilled they were all eating the same meal for a change. She was so weary that once she had announced the fantastic amount of money the centre had raised from the day, she went upstairs for a hot bath.

Rupert went with Celia into the kitchen to help her clear up. He put his arms around her and gave her a kiss.

"I'm so proud of you both Ce,"

"Rupert, I've been a silly snob. Comparing my own unique, quirky daughter with my friend's daughter is unforgivable. To see what Chloe has achieved today has opened my eyes to what a beautiful talented daughter we have." Celia responded to him.

A relieved Rupert replied, "Yes, well I always did say she took after me…!"

With that, Celia picked up the hand towel and playfully hit him on the shoulder with it…

The Training Day

—◊◊◊—

THE ALARM BUZZED on Selina's Android phone which was situated on her bedside cabinet. Selina had been in such a deep sleep. She shot up in bed, sleepily attempting to grab her phone to turn off the alarm, but her hand got caught in the charging wire attached to it. The phone flew onto the floor. 'Great start to the day,' she thought, just as she remembered what the day entailed. 'A training course, oh how much I hate them.'

She retrieved the phone from the floor, turned off the alarm and the several other alarm times she had set. The phone had survived its traumatic fall thanks to its plastic cover.

It was still dark. Selina put on the light and looked in the mirror. Her unruly hair looked like it would need a lot of attention before she left her flat to catch the bus. Selina could drive but she had been warned by friends that any courses at the hotel in the town are best accessed using buses. The hotel car park was very expensive, unless you were staying there. The nearest other car parks were a long walk away from the hotel and would still work out expensive. Selina worked as a locum, meaning she did agency work and was employed at various sites over the country, mainly covering maternity leave or other staff absences. She enjoyed the freedom of being able to pick and choose what work and where she worked. The downside was that she had to organise her own training days, which usually cost her a lot of money, not to mention sometimes losing a day's pay. She couldn't believe her luck with this training day, she saw it online on the Trade Union website, of which she was a member. It was actually free of charge and included lunch. It also fell on a day that she didn't work so it was almost 'Happy Days' except Selina would rather be at home!

She hadn't been on a bus for as long as she could remember. Someone she knew had told her that the bus stop she needed to wait at, was outside the school. She had no idea where bus stops were or even which side of the road to stand.

Once she had washed, dressed, tamed her wild hair and managed a small morsel for breakfast, she set off for the bus stop. It was cold and still fairly dark when she stood at the bus stop with several others. Just as she was studying the other bus passengers, the bus turned up. She watched the others and followed suit, feeling silly that she felt nervous using a bus. Being a locum, she had to drive because most of the work involved home visits to patients. The bus was pretty full so she sat next to a young man, who just carried on looking out of the window. She stood up when he needed to get off. He quickly brushed past her and rang the bell and walked down the moving bus until it stopped. She was pleased that when she was to get off, it was the final stop and she could walk off with the remaining passengers.

Once off the bus, she made the short walk to the hotel. She was half an hour early. The friendly receptionist asked her to pick up a name badge from the nearby table and take a seat until the conference suite was open for attendees.

Within a few minutes some more participants came and sat down next to her. A tall immaculate middle aged lady wearing a name badge with Genevieve on it, sat down opposite Selina.

"Are we all on the dementia course?" she almost shouted at them all.

Selina thought to herself, perhaps a little unkindly; 'Here we go, there's always one. I suppose she's going to get all the answers right and by the end of the day, we will know her life story.'

The others looked at Genevieve and nodded, one or two went back to looking at their phones. Selina smiled and said, "Yes, I'm Selina."

Genevieve smiled, "Yes I know, it's on your badge," she said almost rudely. She continued to talk loudly about her profession and qualifications.

'A me, me, me type,' Selina thought. 'And this is before we even get to the room.'

The facilitator, a friendly lady called Gail, led them up the corridor into the conference room. Selina scurried to get a seat at the back as usual. The idea was that she wouldn't get picked on if she hid at the back. Genevieve went straight to the front. 'No surprises there,' thought Selina.

The room gradually filled up and at nine o'clock prompt, Gail introduced herself and began the housekeeping rules. Selina managed to stifle a yawn. She had heard it all before. Her phone was in her bag, switched on to the silent mode. She listened to the fire instructions, then lost concentration for a few seconds. Flasks of hot water for them to make a hot drink, would be brought into the room at ten fifteen, Gail informed them. They would have a twenty minute comfort break.

'That's me on water then,' Selina thought. 'I can never work those damn flasks.'

After the housekeeping rules, Gail began by explaining her credentials including her vast experience with dementia. Selina was quite impressed by her, well, that made a change. She generally got fed up with going on courses, where some of the facilitators looked like they had just 'Googled' the information and struggled answering any questions with confidence. But in this instance, Gail was showing a great in depth knowledge on the subject. That was when she wasn't interrupted by the 'know all' Genevieve. Selina admired Gail's patience with her.

'Far more patient than I would be.' Selina thought. Selina managed to get to the break, actually concentrating on what Gail was saying. She even managed to contribute, something she rarely did, mainly because she wasn't 'loud' she got ignored, hence gave up bothering.

At the break time, the attendees queued up for drinks. There was a young chap in front of Selina. He turned to Selina.

"Now I've mastered the flask, can I pour some water for you too? I'm hopeless with these things!"

Selina grabbed a cup and opened a sachet of coffee into it, laughing.

"I was just about to grab a bottle of water, rather than show my ignorance with that!"

They both laughed and added some milk to their drinks.

"Thanks James," Selina said looking at his name badge.

They chatted during most of the break until Selina excused herself to go off to the loo.

After the break, Gail went over to the flip chart. Selina thought, 'here we go, we now have to shout out appropriate words. This is where my mind goes blank.'

Yes, they were asked to throw out certain words and to Selina's surprise an amazing word came out of her mouth when she put her hand up. 'Where did that come from?' It was even better than what had come out of Genevieve's mouth, in fact Gail didn't write one word on the flip chart which Genevieve suggested, because they weren't relevant.

Before the lunchtime break, they were all given handouts with questions on and they had to fill out what they thought were appropriate responses, then they had to hand them to the person sitting next to them to look at. There were no right or wrong responses, it was just to create debate. An exercise that gave the participants a chance to think and look at other perspectives to problems. Another exercise that Selina hated. Her mind as usual, went blank and the suitable responses never really sprang to her mind. She was just the same at interviews, she just couldn't think when put on the spot, which is probably why she ended up doing agency work once she qualified. It was probably meant to be, because she enjoyed the variety of the work.

Selina was again pleasantly surprised by actually putting down some reasonable responses. It wasn't a competition to outdo each other, it was just a way of getting the group to interact and appreciate each other's views. Selina noticed that during the discussion 'Miss know-it-all', seemed a bit clueless, although she never managed to keep quiet enough to listen, often turning the discussion back to her life.

Lunchtime arrived, Selina was hot and tired. The room had been very stuffy. They all went down to the restaurant and queued up for a hot lunch. She was at the front of the queue because she had sat at the back of the room, near the exit, so was one of the first out.

Selina took her plate of pasta to a table, picking up the cutlery on the way. She looked up when James asked her if he could join her.

"Yes, sure, how are you finding it?" Selina asked him.

"Better than I thought," he replied. "I dread these courses but they have to be done and I had the added stress of getting a bus here too, something I'm not used to."

"You sound like me, James, I can't remember ever getting a bus into town before."

They both laughed and further into their conversation, they both found out they only lived a mile away from each other. James had only been in the area for around two months.

Just then, Genevieve pulled out her chair and sat next to James.

"Okay if I plonk here?" she announced.

"Of course," James replied.

Selina felt a bit miffed.

Genevieve had quite a big lunch in front of her, so for a few minutes she was quiet as she tucked in. Selina was telling James about the lovely coffee shop near where she lived because he was still new to the area. She was just waiting for Genevieve to butt in, when right on cue she did.

"You both live near the Dementia Centre by the sounds of it?"

James replied to her;

"Yes, not only do I live nearby but I've just taken over as Registered Manager of it!"

"Really?" Selina replied. "I had heard on the grapevine that it was failing and needed new management to turn it around. So you have a job on your hands then?"

"Certainly have, but we can do it. That's why I need all the knowledge I can and why I am here. I heard Gail has a wealth of experience and this course includes governance as well as more valuable information about the illness."

Genevieve was still quietly eating. Selina wondered if she was alright, particularly after the morning's contributions she had made.

Selina asked if she was okay. Genevieve looked sad.

"Yes, I'm sorry, it's just that my husband was at the Dementia Centre for several years until he died."

Selina glanced at James. Genevieve was probably early fifties so either her husband was younger than most to have been diagnosed or he had been a lot older than her. It was as if Genevieve could read her mind.

"He was only fifty five when he was diagnosed. He became violent and I couldn't cope. The ironic thing is that I am a nurse and work in a residential home where most of the residents have dementia. It was felt the best place for Graham was the purpose built Dementia Centre which was new then. I thought he was well cared for and the staff were always lovely when I visited so it was so disappointing that the place was in trouble particularly at the time when Graham died."

James and Selina were at a loss for words. Selina immediately wondered how Genevieve had coped. She admired her for continuing to work in the same field.

'Don't judge a book by its cover' was what then came to Selina's mind. Selina didn't feel guilty about having negative thoughts about Genevieve during the morning because she had just felt irritated by her attitude at the time.

Genevieve broke the silence.

"My daughter thinks I should change from nursing in dementia care and move into another area because she says it's all been too much. I have resisted so far, that's why I'm on the course. But now I'm beginning to think she's right, despite how much experience I have had, I haven't got much right this morning, it's almost like I've lost it."

"Maybe she is right Genevieve, you need to think it over." Selina replied.

The lunch break came to an end and the three of them went back to the conference suite.

There was a speaker for the first hour after lunch, which was very enlightening and Selina took in every word. When the tea break arrived, James poured the hot water onto Selina's teabag in her cup. Selina thanked him for her being able to have the hot drinks that day, she felt sure that if it wasn't for him, she would have just had to stay on water, although not a bad thing.

James chatted with Selina and during the conversation he asked what area she specialised in as a locum.

"Home visits and as most involve someone living with dementia, I thought this course would be appropriate," she explained to him, then quietly added, "not to mention it was free, with lunch thrown in!"

"Mind you, I am getting a bit tired of travelling, sometimes for well over an hour before I even start my day's work, but I enjoy it."

After the break, it was the dreaded role play. They were put into groups. James ended up in the same group with Genevieve. Suprisingly, Selina actually enjoyed being with her group members and working out the scenario and its outcomes, they all worked well together.

Gail spent the last half an hour of the training course rounding up the day's events. Whilst filling out the evaluation form, Selina thought how quiet Genevieve had been all afternoon.

Gail thanked them all for attending and wished everyone a safe journey home.

James caught up with Selina as she took off her name badge ready to put back on the table.

"Can we catch the bus together as we are both bus amateurs?" He joked.

"Yes, of course," Selina replied.

Genevieve rushed up behind them just as they reached the hotel entrance.

"Before you both go, Thanks for listening to me at lunchtime. My daughter is right, it's time for a change. I've learnt a lot from today and it's made me realise that."

James and Selina wished Genevieve well with her new chapter in her life and waved to her as she walked off in one direction. The two of them walked in another direction towards the bus stop.

They chatted on the bus on the way back and both got off the bus together, within walking distance of their own homes. Selina went to speak and say goodbye to James but he got in first.

"Selina, if you do decide you have had enough of travelling around, just come and see me. I'm sure there would be a position at my place, you have the right experience and attitude. You could be such a great asset with helping to get the place to be ran like it should be. We've swapped numbers and you know where I am! It's been great to meet you today though"

He smiled, brushed his wavy hair away from his eyes and waited for her reply.

"I will think about it," she said. "It's nice of you to consider me, although I will have to pass the interview first!" She laughed. He turned to walk home, looked back, winked at her and shouted:

"See you soon!"

Selina walked home with a smile on her face. She was pretty sure she would see him soon. All in all, it had been a very productive day in every way. It clearly had been for James and Genevieve too.

In fact for a training day she was dreading, she could honestly say, she had thoroughly enjoyed it!

Hotel

"IT'S HARD WORK Denise, but you will get used to it!" Stephanie picked the pile of towels from the store cupboard and put on her work trolley. She also put on a box of chocolate wafers and studied the trolley to make sure everything was on it for the day's work.

It was 1978 and Denise was a young seventeen year old starting her first 'proper' job on a Government Training Scheme at the most elite hotel of its time, at the city nearest to her small hometown, ten miles away. The idea of the scheme was for Denise to rotate around the hotel over six months. The plan was for her to do one month in each department. She wondered if that would happen, because even in her young life, she understood 'the best laid plans' saying.

Denise was not work shy and had already had several little part time jobs which fitted around her school work. She had stayed at school to take her 'A' levels but after a few months, got bored and decided she wanted to work and have fun. Because she had no idea of what career path she was going to take, it was suggested by the school that she participated in some kind of training scheme.

Denise followed Stephanie to the first out of fourteen rooms which they were going to service between them. The following day and for the rest of the month she would work on her own. She was just shadowing Stephanie for the day. Stephanie opened the first door and Denise was amazed to see how big it was. Stephanie explained the process to Denise. Everyday, clean sheets were put on the beds; this was a four star hotel and the standards were very high. The room had to be thoroughly cleaned and the bathroom had to sparkle and shine. Finally, the tea tray had to be set out in a certain way, with the packets of chocolate wafers placed neatly on the top of each cup. Stephanie added that each day, the housekeeper would pick a random room to check by each chambermaid and they would reprimand the chambermaid if the room was not up to the expected standards. The housekeeper would run her finger over tops of wardrobes to check for dust, check beds were made properly, bathrooms with no smears and the tea tray with everything put in place. Denise and Stephanie worked hard all day. It was certainly an eye opener to Denise on the world of work. The eight hour day was exhausting for Denise, making the two hour shifts in the local Wimpy Bar she used to do after school seem very lightweight in comparison.

By Friday, Denise travelled home on the bus at the end of the final shift for the week. She was exhausted and looking forward to a weekend of rest before she set off at seven o'clock on Monday morning for the start of the second week. Because she was on a training scheme she was allowed to work Monday to Friday whilst chambermaiding but when she started work in another area, she would have to work different hours.

On Monday morning of her second week, Denise arrived at the hotel, pleased to be in the warm after getting cold waiting at the bus stop and walking to the hotel. Light snowflakes had started to fall as she stood under the bus shelter. By the time she got off the bus, the snow had settled but the forecast was for it to clear up later.

She began her work on the eighth floor that day. When it got to eleven o'clock, she stopped for a drink of water and ate one of the chocolate wafers out of the box off her trolley. She wasn't sure whether it was allowed but the other chambermaids ate them so she just followed what they did. She went to the window which stretched the full length of the room. She noticed from looking down at the pavement that the snow had turned to slush but the day was very grey. It was a lovely view over the city. Across the road from the hotel were offices where she noticed a man, a middle aged looking man wearing a woolly hat standing outside one of the office entrances. For some reason she thought he looked shifty, then she thought better of it. 'How can you tell if someone looks shifty from this height, you daft thing?' she thought. 'Anyway, I must get back to work, I've still got lots more rooms to service.'

After four weeks, Denise expected to move to the kitchen, however a chambermaid was still on the sick so she was asked to do another few weeks. Denise was happy in some ways, she quite liked working alone in the hotel rooms, she put the radio on for company and the hotel was nice and warm. She did feel though, that she was being used as free labour for the hotel, and she was there to learn and build up skills, not just clean and make beds.

One day, six weeks after Denise started at the hotel, she was asked by a manager to work in the carvery restaurant from the following Monday. It meant working in the evenings, so she was offered a staff room for the rest of her time there. She was pleased because the hard work and the travelling was very tiring, particularly as it was February and freezing cold outside.

On Monday, Denise arrived at the hotel in plenty of time to settle in the room before she started her first shift in the Carvery restaurant. She thought the small room was very nice. It had a sink and toilet in it. There was a shower room at the end of the corridor. The staff rooms were at the back of the hotel so the view from the room was pretty bleak. Just a car park and bins.

She thoroughly enjoyed the first evening in the restaurant. She was given her own set of tables to look after. The chefs served the meat and the customers then added their own vegetables from the vast and delicious looking choices. Denise welcomed customers and served their starters, desserts and drinks. She had to take all the dirty dishes to the kitchen where she was slightly nervous of the German head chef especially when he was swearing loudly. The waitresses were allowed to keep their tips so Denise was very happy at the end of the shift when she counted the money she had made that night. It certainly boosted the pittance of pay she was receiving from the British Government.

A few days later, Denise was due to begin work at five o'clock that night. She spent most of the morning asleep in bed because she hadn't gone to bed until three o'clock in the morning. Some of the waitresses and chefs went out after work and they invited her to join them. Denise had a great time, even though she wasn't legally allowed to be in the bar, but this was 1978 and there was no such thing as an ID. The bouncers on the door may sometimes ask a person their age but just had to take the person's word that they were the age they said. Denise was beginning to love living in the hotel, in the centre of a lively city, it was so much fun.

Denise had a shower and went to the canteen for a snack then went back to her room. She had a couple of hours to kill before work so she laid on the bed and read a magazine. At four o'clock she looked out her window, it was another miserable February day. A man in the staff car park below caught her eye. She thought he looked familiar, then she remembered where she had seen him before. It was from one of the windows at the front of the hotel when she was working as a chambermaid. The middle aged man with the woolly hat who she thought looked 'shifty'. She watched him and he moved from near the entrance to the car park to right at the entrance. He wasn't doing anything other than standing there but Denise was convinced he looked like he was up to something. She went back to her magazine for a while, then put on a bit of makeup before she took the lift down to the Carvery to begin work.

The very next day, Denise heard one of the waitresses talking to a chef whilst the chef was putting the meats out on display for when the restaurant opened. The chef said his car had been broken in to the previous day. Denise busied herself near them so she could hear the rest of the conversation. She decided that the 'shifty' man was responsible, she knew he was up to no good lurking around. The chef had his cassette player stolen from his car, she heard him say. Denise stood there for a moment daydreaming, when suddenly the head chef made her jump.

"We are open now Denise, and look at who has just sat at one of your tables."

Denise looked at him and for once he was smiling, but she looked across at the table and had no idea who the middle aged gentleman who sat alone on the table was.

"Can I get you a drink Sir?" she asked him when she reached his table.

Denise took his order and walked off towards the bar to fetch the drink. The chef nipped away from his carving area to her and said he couldn't believe she was serving Billy Wright. He briefly explained he was a football legend. Denise picked up the tray with the drink on and hurried off. She had no idea about football and had never heard of him. There had been many famous people staying at the hotel since she had been there but Denise had rarely heard of any of them. She did speak to Ken Dodd after she serviced his room and the only reason why she had heard of him was because her father was a fan of his. Ken Dodd was staying there for many weeks whilst he was in the pantomime at the local theatre. Most of the time Denise did not get fazed by these people mainly because they were unknown to her. She thought it was quite funny that the chefs were so excited by this one man called Billy. He was a very nice man though, she thought as she looked after him that evening. Apparently he was married to one of the Beverley Sisters, another chef told her. 'Who on earth are the Beverley Sisters?' she thought.

It had been a very busy evening. It was past midnight before Denise finally got to bed. She wasn't tired and kept thinking of that man she had seen that she was convinced was a thief. She made a decision to go to the police the next day and report him. She had a good description of him.

The following morning, Denise left the hotel and set off for the local police station. She hadn't mentioned any of this to her work colleagues. She didn't feel she could as she had no real close friends there because of the short time she had worked there. Once in the police station she told the man behind the desk about the 'shifty' man. To her surprise the man laughed at her, explaining that she had no evidence that the man had done anything wrong. She hadn't seen him touch any of the cars. She felt he was laughing at her because she was young and he wasn't taking her seriously.

"You have to have evidence, love," he said to her. "You stick to your waitressing."

Denise was annoyed that he treated her like a child and was patronising. She glared at him and left feeling downhearted because she knew she was right and now others may get something stolen because she wasn't taken seriously.

Denise had another few weeks in the Carvery restaurant before she moved into another department. The lady from the personnel department informed her that she would work morning and evening shifts in the kitchen. Denise was happy to move even though she loved the Carvery, but she was nervous about being in the kitchen with the head chef. The first shift started at seven in the morning. She worked with a lovely middle aged lady who showed her everything that was required of her. It involved making sandwiches and breakfasts for room service. Putting them on the dummy waiter then getting in the lift to the appropriate floor, fetching the tray from the dummy waiter and delivering to the appropriate room. Room service was twenty four hours with airline pilots able to have breakfast delivered at any time due to their unsociable working hours.

The next day she worked the late shift which started at two o'clock in the afternoon. This included making the starters for the A La Carte restaurant. It was certainly all go, she never stopped.

After working six days on the trot, she had a couple of days off and she had been asked by some of the kitchen staff if she wanted to go out with them to a club on the evening of the first day off. She thought she would go into the city centre during the day and buy some new clothes with the tips she had made working in the Carvery.

On the evening that she was meeting up with the others, Denise put on her new black leather look trousers and new top.

She looked quite nice, she thought to herself and she definitely looked older than she was, now she had makeup on and nice clothes. She picked up her bag and set off down to the busy reception area to meet the others.

They all went to a bar, then moved on to a nightclub. Denise really enjoyed herself and danced with the others to hits like The Bee Gees *Night Fever* and Chic's *Everybody Dance*. She was so pleased she was able to live in the hotel and have fun on her days off!

Towards the end of the evening an exhausted Denise sat down and sipped her drink. The others were still dancing. She looked towards the nearby bar and noticed a man walking up to the bar. He stood out because he was middle aged and had a hat on. 'Goodness,' she thought. 'It's that shifty man who hangs around the hotel.' She watched him and to her horror, he helped himself to a wallet out of a young chap's back pocket. She sat frozen to her seat as he just walked off into the darkness and the young chap disappeared into the crowd. She decided there was nothing she could do. The man at the police station reception had taken no notice of her.

"Come on Den, come and have a dance with me!" One of her work friends grabbed her arm and whisked her onto the dance floor where they danced solidly for at least the next half an hour.

The next day when Denise came round about lunchtime, the first thing that came into her mind was the 'shifty' man. 'Right,' she thought. 'I am going to go back to the police station and tell them. I have the evidence now.'

She showered, then went to the canteen and had a cheese salad sandwich and a glass of water. She then walked to the police station. When she entered, it was the same man at the reception. She told him she was out with her work colleagues from the hotel for an evening out and how she saw the pickpocket. She reminded him that she had been before to report the man, but had no evidence of a crime being committed but she had now. He just stared at her.

"May I ask what you were doing at that nightclub? You certainly don't look twenty one to me."

Denise went hot. She hadn't thought about being under age in the nightclub.

"Look, okay I was too young to be at the club, but there was a crime committed."

"Oh, and you didn't commit a crime then?" he glared at her.

"Oh whatever." She turned to go, feeling stupid that she had forgot about being under age in the club, but also feeling annoyed that she just wasn't being taken seriously.

"Excuse me Miss, I still need details of the man and I want your name and address for our records, before you go."

Denise gave a full detailed description of the pickpocket, then reluctantly gave him her name and the hotel name.

She left and walked slowly back to the hotel. She could kick herself for taking notice of the man when he was loitering around the hotel and almost wished she hadn't seen the pickpocket. She felt really fed up for the rest of her day off.

The weeks passed and Denise soon forgot her bad 'Police Station' experiences. She finished her work in the kitchen and moved to work on the Penthouse floor. It was the top floor and they held conferences and banquets. There were also several penthouse suites. It was a very busy time for Denise, she never stopped for a second on the long shifts. Taking coffee into business meetings, preparing for banquets, cleaning the penthouse suites as well as looking out for famous people, most she had never heard of because of her young age. She did recognise Gilbert

O'Sullivan who was very popular in the 1970's. She was thrilled that he spoke to her.

One day, the manager approached her whilst she was just preparing the coffee trolley for some business people. He smiled at her.

"Hi Denise, there is a policeman downstairs at the reception, he would like to speak to you. Don't worry about the coffee, I will find someone else to do it. You just go."

Denise felt complete panic inside. She assumed they wanted to talk to her about being under age in a nightclub. What would her parents say? Her legs were shaking as she entered the lift. When she walked from it on the ground floor, she saw the police officer. He smiled at her as she walked towards him.

"Don't look so worried!" he said to her.

They sat down and to her surprise he thanked her for such a detailed description of the man who had stolen the wallet. He had gone on to commit further crimes and together with her description and other evidence they were able to make an arrest, charge him and he has been sentenced at the Magistrates Court. The officer did add that she should only attend night clubs when she was old enough. Licence holders could lose their licences for serving under age people, he told her. They had a bit more friendly chat, said their goodbyes, then Denise got back into the lift to finish her day's work.

She breathed a sigh of relief when the lift doors closed.

Later that evening, an exhausted Denise lay on her bed thinking. She only had a few weeks left of her six month training scheme. In some ways she was glad because she couldn't go out with the others anymore for nights out, but she would miss the work and the friendly work colleagues.

She realised that she had nearly got herself into serious

trouble but as soon as she finished at the hotel…her future was going to be in the Police Force.

By 1998 Denise had worked her way up through the ranks and had just received an award for outstanding detective work on a high profile case. As she sat on her sofa at the home she shared with her husband and children, she looked proudly at the medal and reflected on how her career started. She thought back to her time at the hotel, the hard work, her detective work and how it set her up for what she had achieved.

'But it was also such fun,' she thought.

'Despite my ermm being a little too young to be clubbing, I did look good in my Olivia Newton John skinny leather look trousers…never lose your sense of humour…!'

Angels

—⚉—

"RIGHT, LILY, EVERYTHING is now packed in Esmeralda. We should be ready to set off first thing in the morning, we've only got to put in the cool box and the rest of the food in, just before we leave." Jeffrey said as he walked into the kitchen where Lily was busy preparing the evening meal.

Esmeralda was the couple's small, old, but so far, trustworthy campervan. They began touring around England and Scotland when Jeffrey retired from his business. Lily was still working with just a few years left as a part time occupational therapist, working at their local social services office.

This latest adventure would begin with a six hour trip up to Western Scotland where they had booked various campsites, working their way up the coast towards Ayr. Although Jeffrey was retired he was still a Councillor on the local council, so their travels fitted around the meetings, as well as Lily's job. This break was slightly longer than usual, ten days with four different campsites.

Harry and Henry, their two rescue spaniels, were sitting on their doggie beds in the corner of the kitchen when Jeffrey chatted with Lily. They looked at each other as if to say 'here we go again'. Once the cool box was brought out, given a wipe over and put on the kitchen table, they knew they would soon be off. They recognised the signs.

The dogs did enjoy travelling around, jumping in and out of the van and sleeping in their crates as the couple took it in turns to drive. Like their mummy and daddy, they enjoyed different scenery, different smells and best of all lots of different furry friends and humans to talk to on their walks.

Lily had been very busy during her last day at work for a fortnight. She had to make sure all the loose ends were tied up by making phone calls, finishing reports and generally rushing around the locality, checking some Disabled Facilities Grant work which had been recently completed, mainly wet rooms.

They both sat down to eat the vegetable risotto and chatted happily about the things they were going to do on their travels. Once they had finished, Jeffrey washed the dishes, whilst Lily fed the dogs.

The next morning they set off as soon as they were ready. They had a couple of stops on the way and reached the campsite near to the Isle of Whithorn by teatime. They walked the dogs, put their fold up chairs on the grass, ate the snacks they had brought with them in the cool box and enjoyed a glass of wine each. They were all tucked up in their snug campervan by nine o'clock.

The next morning, Jeffrey and Lily were up at six o'clock. They took it in turns to use the immaculate facilities to shower and dress, then took a dog each for their morning walk. They enjoyed the warm summer day, where they walked and admired the spectacular views around the Isle of Whithorn. The next day they set off to the Mull of Galloway. A friend of theirs had talked about the stunning scenery and fabulous views, where you could see various islands on a clear day. They were both overawed by the area, from the road leading up to it, to the place itself. They were just simply amazed by what they saw. Even their friend's vivid description didn't do it justice, it was one of those places that had to be seen to be believed. They took endless photos, all complimented by the cloudless blue sky. Lily went into the cafe and brought some takeaway coffee and scones complete with jam and cream. She took them back to Jeffrey at the campervan. Jeffrey was sitting inside with the dogs by his side, admiring the scenes from the open sliding door. By late afternoon, they set off towards Stranraer, where just two miles on from there, was the campsite which they had booked for two nights. They took the scenic route and enjoyed the 'wilderness' of it all. Little cottages dotted about and farm animals filling the fields. Jeffery was just taking a sharp bend when the unexpected happened. Emeralda lost power and Jeffrey had no other option than to steer her into the gateway of what looked like a dilapidated bungalow, which he just managed before she conked out.

They both looked at eachother.

"What on earth has happened?" Jeffrey looked at Lily.

"It's not long been serviced has it? Lily replied.

Jeffrey got out and tinkered around and realised there was nothing he could do apart from ring the breakdown company. They called the camp site to let them know they wouldn't make it before the check in time closed. Unfortunately, a barrier came down at closing time and without the key fob which they would have picked up on arrival, they wouldn't be able to get in until the next day.

"It's a good job the bungalow is not lived in," Jeffrey said to Lily who was busy feeding both the dogs.

"It is, we wouldn't be very popular if it was! Sleeping in someone's gateway is not what we planned, but at least no one is around."

They had been warned it may be quite a wait until the breakdown company came out, so they made themselves a snack and a hot drink, using the last bit of boiling water from their flask.

Eventually, the breakdown company arrived and Jeffrey explained to the chap what had happened. Lily sat in the van, sliding door open, looking at the beautiful sunset, wishing she was at the campsite. She glanced at the bungalow, then realised that a light was switched on.

'Oh no, someone lives there,' she thought. 'It doesn't look habitable, surely not.'

She had no choice but to go and find out, after all they were parked in the gateway. The dogs were curled up together in a crate at the back of the van, Jeffrey was with the breakdown man, so she just walked down the short overgrown driveway and knocked on the door. She stood on the doorstep for at least five minutes until the door opened. She couldn't believe what she saw. A tiny wizened, unkempt, elderly lady stood there wearing a tatty night dress. Lily explained what had happened. The frail lady invited her in. Lily followed her along a short cluttered hallway. The house smelt musty and unclean. The lounge was a couple of steps down from the hallway and Lily noticed the kitchen, which went off from the lounge, had another couple of steps going down to it. It took several minutes for the lady to manage the steps; there was no handrail.

"Have a wee sit down," the lady pointed to a chair.

Lily couldn't sit down, the couple of rickety armchairs were laden with clutter. The little old lady sat down on the only armchair that was free from clutter, and put a dirty blanket over her knees.

"I'm so sorry to have disturbed you, my name is Lily and my husband is called Jeffrey."

"That's fine, my dear. I'm Morag. Do you want a cup of tea?"

Lily nodded, smiled at Morag and diplomatically refused.

"If you don't mind Morag, would we be able to have some water because it looks like we will be sleeping in your gateway tonight."

"Of course, dear. Just bring your bottle in to fill."

The two women chatted for a short while, where Lily learnt that Morag had no relatives that she knew of and had never married. She was totally alert mentally, but physically it was clear she could not look after herself anymore. Lily popped back to the campervan only to find Jeffrey sitting outside with Harry and Henry.

"Where is the breakdown man?"

"He's gone, but he's going to contact the garage to arrange for a part. The trouble is that it is Sunday tomorrow! At this rate we could be camping here for two nights."

Lily explained about Morag, to Jeffrey's surprise, who couldn't believe that anyone could live in the place. Lily picked up her water bottle, kettle and flask. They would have no electric hook up so she would see if she could boil her kettle in Morag's and fill the flask. Luckily, they were well stocked in the campervan and thankfully they had a portaloo.

Lily went back into the bungalow and explained to Morag about boiling the kettle. She took the couple of steps down to the kitchen and found it very dirty, with no evidence of any recent food preparation. She decided to pop back to the van whilst the kettle was boiling and bring back some milk to make

Morag a drink. When she went back to the kitchen, she filled the washing up bowl with hot soapy water and washed a few dishes and quickly wiped around the draining board. She filled her flask, then made 3 cups of tea, using teabags from their stocks. She took one outside to Jeffrey, then picked up some other bits from inside the van and returned to the kitchen. She found out how Morag's grill worked, toasted some bread, then buttered it and topped it with raspberry jam. All from the stocks in the campervan. She took Morag the hot toast and cup of tea. Morag wolfed down the toast and drank every bit of the tea, like she hadn't eaten or drank properly for a while.

'Bless her,' Lily thought to herself, before taking her things back to the campervan. It was quite late, so Lily prepared a simple snack and they both sat outside in the warm air. Lily cleared up whilst Jeffrey walked both dogs, then they both sat for a while longer with a glass of rose wine, reflecting on the fact that they were sitting in a gateway, rather than at the campsite. Luckily, it was a full moon, so it made it quite a pleasant evening outside and they had battery operated lights for inside the van.

Despite the unusual surroundings, both Jeffrey and Lily slept well in the campervan. They were both up early, having washed the best they could with their limited water, obviously missing the luxury of campsite facilities. They had some fruit juice and cereal before walking the dogs and then sat inside the van and chatted about Morag. They both knew they had to do something to help Morag particularly as they were likely to be still parked in her gateway for at least another night. Once they had put their bedding away and tidied up their breakfast dishes, they put the dogs in their crates in the van for a sleep and both went to see Morag. Morag took a while to open the door, still in the same old, tatty nightdress. They slowly followed Morag to the lounge, with Lily carrying their kettle and flask. Jeffrey chatted with Morag whilst Lily boiled the kettle and filled their flask. She then reboiled it and made Morag a hot chocolate made from what she found in Morag's cupboard. She looked in the fridge, there was very little in it but as they were well stocked in the campervan, Lily nipped back for some supplies. She soon rustled up some cereal and toast with jam for Morag, then with the mugs she had brought from the campervan, took the opportunity to make a hot drink for both of them.

Whilst Lily had been busy, Jeffrey found out that Morag had lived in the bungalow since birth. It had been her parents' bungalow. She lived alone after her parents passed away and eventually married but was widowed when she was fifty and had lived alone ever since. She had no children and no family. When Lily brought in the drinks, she asked Morag how she shopped. Her reply was that the milkman delivered groceries, a limited supply.

Lily decided to just dive in and ask Morag if she would like some help with a shower. To her surprise Morag agreed. It just meant that Lily had to go and clean up the bathroom before they started, but it gave her something to do. Neither she or Jeffrey could do much else until their pick up truck came the following day to pick up Esmeralda and take them to a garage in Stranraer. Whilst Lily was assisting Morag with her shower, Jeffery took advantage of the electricity and charged up the mobile phone. He looked around the outside of the bungalow and did a few jobs outside, just to tidy up a bit.

When he went back inside Morag was dressed in a clean dress and Lily had washed and dried her hair. She was totally transformed and looked several years younger.

"Morag, would you mind if we called social services to arrange a little help for you?" Jeffrey asked her.

Morag looked at him and thought for a few minutes.

"Maybe, I do need a wee bit of help."

Jeffrey removed his phone from the charger and looked up the social services number. He wasn't sure if there was any difference in services in Scotland than what he and Lily knew in England, but he would find out.

After a long wait, he was put through to the out of hours team as it was the weekend. An urgent assessment was scheduled for the following Thursday, although he would have preferred it to have been sooner because he classed Morag's situation as urgent. He explained what he and Lily thought would be needed including some minor adaptations and a lot of daily support.

The rest of the day was spent with Lily cleaning, washing some of Morag's clothes and making some meals from their campervan supplies. Jeffrey carried on with some repair work. The dogs came into the bungalow and Morag loved stroking them. They wandered around the enclosed garden whilst Jeffrey worked. Both Jeffrey and Lily felt exhausted by late evening, and although they could have a good wash, both felt in desperate need of a shower. Both of them and their dogs were all asleep by ten o'clock that night.

They were up very early the next morning. They walked and fed Harry and Henry and put them in their crates whilst they had their breakfast. They took their mugs to Morag's bungalow to make themselves and Morag hot drinks. There was enough time for Morag to eat her breakfast and Lily to assist her with a shower and getting dressed. Just as they were finishing off, the pick up truck arrived. The idea was that the couple rode in the cab with the driver and the campervan was put on the truck.

"Jeffrey, I want to come back here on Thursday and make sure that the assessment is done thoroughly. I want them to know how we found Morag and that she gets the help she needs."

"But Lily, we are on holiday! Although it's not as planned so far!" Jeffrey replied as the pick up truck was reversing into position. But he knew what Lily was like, she wouldn't enjoy the rest of the holiday if she didn't check that Morag was being looked after and he too had grown very fond of Morag in the short time they had spent with her.

"Okay, Lily, we will drive down on Thursday for the assessment which is at two o'clock, as long as you promise to enjoy the next few days."

Lily kissed Jeffrey's cheek.

They both went into the lounge to say their goodbyes to Morag.

"Are you happy for us to join you when you have your assessment on Thursday Morag?"

Lily knelt next to Morag holding her tiny hand. How different she looked now she was showered, hair washed and wearing clean clothes. Such a difference from two days ago. The bungalow was also now a bit cleaner, if only in the kitchen and bathroom.

"My dears, you are angels, I can't thank you enough. I would love you both to be here, but you can't ruin any more of your holiday."

"It won't, we'll see you on Thursday."

They both hugged her and left quickly because they all felt a little emotional.

Jeffrey and Lily spent the morning in Stranraer with the dogs, whilst Esmeralda was being fixed. It took about three hours, so they sat outside a coffee house in the town centre and enjoyed a cappuccino and a cake each, with the dogs seeking out any dropped crumbs.

Once Esmeralda was repaired, Jeffrey drove her just out of town on the A77 and pulled up at a lay-by.

"Just there," Jeffrey pointed to an adjoining campsite. "Is where we should have camped the past few nights."

They both looked at the site which had a lovely outlook onto the water and felt disappointed that they had missed their two nights.

"Oh well, let's just look forward to our next few nights," Lily replied.

They set off towards Girvan, near to where their next four nights were to be spent. Jeffrey reckoned it would probably take about an hour and a half to get back to Morag on Thursday. The couple and their two dogs spent the next few days visiting the beautiful beaches and admiring the scenery including the landmark island, Ailsa Craig, famous for granite used to make curling stones.

Finally, Thursday arrived and they all set off back to Morag's bungalow. Morag was delighted to see them again. Lily had enough time to help Morag into some fresh clothes. The social services assessor arrived on time and Morag gave her permission for the couple to be there to support her. The dogs came in as well and settled down on Morag's threadbare carpet. The questions were endless, so Lily, who had bought a few supplies with her, made some tea and put out some biscuits.

"Have you any relatives at all?" the assessor asked Morag.

"No dear, I did have a brother, he was called Billy MacMicking. That was my maiden name by the way," Morag smiled.

"Billy was always in trouble and he left home in disgrace, moved to England and I have never seen him again. I heard a rumour that he had some children, but I really don't know anything else."

The conversations carried on and finally several hours later, a plan was worked out on how to help Morag with a package of care support starting within days. A keysafe, to be situated on the wall outside the front door, would be fitted the very next day.

As soon as the couple and their dogs were settled in Esmeralda for the journey back to their site, Jeffrey glanced at Lily.

"You know what Lily, there is an officer on my council, called Alastair MacMicking. How weird is that? When Morag said her brother's name I was startled."

They both chatted all the way back about the assessment. Pleased that some care support would be starting and also there would be an assessment around the home for minor adaptations. They were still both concerned about the state of the bungalow but there was only so much they could help with. The assessor had got their details and was prepared to keep in touch with Morag's blessing.

The couple and their two dogs went on to enjoy the last few days of their holiday, and Esmeralda behaved herself for the rest of the trip.

Things settled back into the normal routine.

One day, two weeks after the couple had returned from their holiday, Jeffrey went to a meeting at the council offices. He had arranged an appointment with an environmental health officer after the meeting, to discuss a matter brought to his attention by a constituent. The meeting lasted about an hour so afterwards he went up a couple of flights of stairs for the appointment. He discussed the constituents' problem with the environmental health officer, and was just about to leave after he had received a satisfactory explanation to the problem, when he noticed Alastair MacMicking, another environmental health officer, working at his desk.

"Hi Alastair, sorry to bother you but can I just have a quick word?"

Alastair took his eyes off his computer screen.

"Of course Jeffrey, bring a chair up."

Jeffrey, aware that this was office time and Alastair was busy working, very briefly discussed meeting Morag.

Alastair looked visibly shocked, so much so that Jeffrey regretted bringing it up, especially at work. He didn't think for one moment that they could be related, just that they had such an unusual name. It was literally a spur of the moment thing. Finally, Alastair spoke.

"You know what Jeffrey, my late father, was called Billy. He did leave Scotland as a teenager because he had done wrong things. He never talked about his family, we never asked because he was a great father, and my mother came from a large family, so we had loads of relatives on her side. Dad did very well considering he came to England with nothing and had been in trouble. He built up a good business and my sister and I never wanted for anything. So now it seems I have an auntie, well that's all good! Not sure why dad never kept in touch with his sister, but I think it's because he just wanted to put that chapter of his life behind him…Wow, though!"

Jeffrey felt relieved by his reply.

"Alastair, I can't keep you from work anymore. I will email you what I can about the situation with her." Alastair stood up and shook Jeffreys hand and thanked him, then attempted to carry on working for the last half an hour or so of the working day.

Jeffrey went home to the two dogs, fed them and was just beginning to prepare the evening meal when Lily walked in. He updated her on the afternoon's events.

"You know Lily, I really didn't think he would be Morag's nephew, it would be too much of a coincidence. I just wanted him to know that we had met someone else with such an unusual name."

The very next day, Jeffrey received an update about Morag's care and how it was now three calls from the care company daily, instead of the two, to ensure she was well supported. Whilst he was still on the phone to social services, he informed them about finding Morag's nephew. The call handler agreed to discuss the news with the manager.

Two days later, Jeffrey received a phone call from the Scottish social services. They had discussed with Morag about her new found nephew and she was absolutely delighted and hoped she could meet him one day. Jeffrey was so pleased when he put the phone down. He went straight to his desk and emailed Alastair with a brief message and a contact number at the social services department he was given. It was now out of his hands and up to Alastair to decide what he wanted to do.

Jeffrey and Lily had made up their minds to book a few more nights in Western Scotland because they loved it up there. So a couple of months later they set off in Esmeralda for their first stay at a campsite near Portpatrick. They had already decided to visit Morag, after all there was no way they could be so close and not visit, and besides they just loved the lady. They had only spoken with her a few times since they returned, mainly because they didn't want to call when her carers were there and they felt she was now in good hands.

They settled at the campsite where they had booked four nights. This time they bought the awning with them. It was an awning they could leave up and drive away from. The weather was calm and warm with a gentle breeze. It was good to be back. On the second day after they had showered, walked the dogs and eaten breakfast, they set off to see Morag. They pulled up in the gateway but this time Esmeralda behaved herself. They put their dogs on their leads and opened the gate to walk down the path towards the bungalow. The couple looked at each other in amazement. The bungalow was transformed. It had been painted and the garden tidied up. Morag knew roughly the time they were coming so had asked the morning carer to leave the door open. They both walked in to Morag sitting in the lounge, Despite her age, she looked years younger than when they first met her. She was wearing a pretty dress, tights and slippers. Both of them hugged her and then sat down. The dogs lay down on a new carpet.

"I said you were angels and you most definitely are," she said to them.

"Alastair has been to visit me. He and his family are wonderful. I never thought I would see any of Billy's family. I'm sad I can't see Billy, but I see him in Alastair. He arranged for the bungalow to be painted and new carpets. Because of his knowledge from the council he has applied to the council here for a grant for a new boiler. I can't thank you both enough."

Morag picked a box off the table next to her chair.

"This is a wee present for you both. I have had them since I was a wee girl but they are yours now."

Lily took the box from Morag's frail hands, sat down and opened it.

Inside was a pair of beautiful angels. Lily had never seen angels that looked so beautiful. They had been handmade and painted to perfection. They had been loved and cherished. Lily didn't want Morag to give them anything, particularly something so sentimental, but she knew Morag wouldn't take no for an answer, so they would both treasure them.

When they left Morag, before her lunchtime care call. The pair walked hand in hand with their dogs back to Esmeralda.

They put the dogs into their crates in the back and both got into the front. Jeffrey put the angels on the dashboard resting safely against the window and quietly, they both looked at them.

"We aren't angels, Lily, we've just been put on this earth to help others when we can."

Despite Esmeraldas doors and windows being closed, there was a sudden dip in the temperature and a cool breeze surrounding them followed by a warm, comfortable, loving presence. Then from nowhere, a white feather floated down and landed near the angels.

Both Lily and Jeffrey looked at each other in astonishment and just as their eyes met, they each felt like they were being hugged, but clearly they weren't.

They smiled at each other, Jeffrey started Esmeralda's engine and they set off back to the campsite.

The angels were now with them…keeping this loving, caring couple …warm and safe.

Girlie Weekend

—⁓—

TINA PARKED HER small Hyundai car in the car park of the hotel on the front overlooking the River Mersey at Liverpool's Albert Dock.

"Well done Tina darling, driving all that way, you can relax now sweetie and we'll treat you to a few drinks in a bit." gushed Pamela, who was sitting in the passenger seat, looking at Tina as she spoke.

"Yes, we sure will Tina," Gillian piped up from the back seat.

Tina, Pamela and Gillian had been friends from their school days. The three of them didn't live near each other anymore but they all lived in the same county, so they weren't hundreds of miles apart. They were all busy ladies so they didn't get to meet up much, but always squeezed in a 'girlie weekend' away each year.

Pamela was born in Barbados and had lived in England since she was five, when her family came over to settle. Gillian was born in England although her parents were Chinese. Her father had spent his working life running a Chinese restaurant/takeaway in the town where they all lived when they were children. Tina was born to British parents and when she was a child used to enjoy going to her friends house for tea after school, where she tasted the different types of cuisine to what she was used to at her home. All three of them loved fashion. Pamela would often sport exotic wigs and striking bright dresses, she was so extrovert, colourful, bubbly and such great fun. Gillian liked subtle colours and was comfortable in neat tailored trousers with matching blouses and fitted jackets. Tina loved her jeans, trendy jackets and boots. Pamela had a partner who was from Zimbabwe and they had a child between them. Gillian was single after breaking up with her partner several years before and Tina was married with two teenage children.

The three of them lifted their cases from the car and checked in at the hotel. They all had a single room each, so arranged to meet down in the bar around half an hour later. They had a quiet evening with a meal and a few drinks in the hotel then had an early night. This was so they were refreshed enough for the busy Saturday where they planned to hit the town early in the morning, before taking the pre-booked ferry trip on the Mersey. All three of them were in good spirits and looking forward to spending the next two days having fun before they would set off home on Monday morning.

Pamela and Tina both slept very well, but it was not the same for Gillian. She had got ready for bed and watched a bit of TV from her bed before drifting off to sleep. In the early hours she suddenly woke up with a start, for a second she wondered where she was, then remembered. She looked around in the dark and saw something. As she blinked hard to convince herself she was awake, she saw a shadow at the end of the bed. As her eyes adjusted to the shadow, she realised it was the outline of a man, who, when she looked more closely, resembled an old fashioned sailor. For some reason she didn't feel frightened, in fact a feeling of warmth came over. She noticed from his faint features that he was Chinese looking. He wrapped his arms around his waist, like he was hugging himself, then slowly faded away. Gillian sat in her bed watching until every trace of this Chinese sailor man had disappeared. She wasn't unnerved, and soon went back into a deep sleep until the alarm on her phone woke her up. Gillian only used her phone to WhatsApp friends and family, make and receive phone calls and as an alarm clock. She did not do Facebook or Twitter since she had broken up with her partner. She remained private and did not want to read about other people's antics anymore. She spent her spare time gardening, keeping fit, the odd coffee with friends and reading. She had made up her mind she did not want to get into another relationship, at least not in the foreseeable future.

Gillian got up as soon as she switched off the alarm and had a quick shower. She thought about the sailor man. It definitely wasn't a figment of her imagination, but she decided not to mention it to the other two. She would put it out of her mind and enjoy the day.

She met the other two in the restaurant where a buffet breakfast was available. Pamela went up first to fetch her breakfast and returned with a very Caribbean type breakfast, full of fruit and colourful, just like Pamela was. Despite it only being eight thirty in the morning, Pamela as usual looked stunning. She was a curvy build and the wig she had put on with its vibrant hair band looked amazing. She wore a calf length dress, full of different shades of yellow and orange with a large green belt which complemented her waist. Tina went up next to fetch a couple of croissants and jam. She was wearing a checked shirt, matching body warmer together with her trademark jeans, tucked into beautiful furry boots. Lastly, Gillian went up to the buffet looking very demure in her simple jumper and smart trousers, finished off with some black, comfortable dolly shoes. The three of them chatted together whilst they ate before setting off from the Albert Dock across the busy main road to the shops. They spent hours browsing around the shops, stopping for coffee before heading back to the hotel to freshen up and drop off their purchases. After a light lunch in a cafe on the Albert Dock, they walked to the Pier Head to catch the Mersey ferry. They took their seats on the ferry. There was a man on the seat next to Pamela. He looked to be of Chinese origin. Pamela in her normal, larger than life way, smiled at the chap.

"Hiya babe, Hope you don't mind being with us noisy ladies."

"You speak for yourself Pamela, Gillian and I are very quiet!" Tina joked with her.

The man smiled at all three of them.

"It's nice to meet you all, I'm Joe by the way. I'm local and work long hours but my mate steers this ferry so he invited me along for the trip today, before I get back to work later."

The four of them chatted amongst themselves at times during the trip. At one point, Gillian and Joe's eyes met for a few seconds, before they both looked the other way. It's understandable, thought Gillian as we both have the same origin. She did think how nice he looked, such a pleasant smile, and touches of grey in the sides of his jet black shiny hair. As the trip ended, Pamela asked Joe if he wanted to join them for a drink at the nearest cafe. He didn't have much time before he had to get back to work but agreed to have a quick cup of tea with them. Once they had finished their drinks, Joe asked the ladies if they were on Facebook, which Pamela and Tina were, so they added Joe as a friend. He looked disappointed when Gillian said she didn't do social media anymore. They all left the cafe, wished Joe well and they went their separate ways.

The ladies walked back to the hotel and prepared themselves for a night on the town. The evening started with a meal in the town, then they set off to a nightclub, returning to the hotel just after midnight. Pamela said they must be getting old as previous years, they had not returned much before two in the morning!

Gillian flopped into her bed around half past midnight and dropped off to sleep more or less straightaway only to be woken up with a start again. It was a repeat of the previous night where she saw the Chinese old fashioned looking sailor. She waited until he disappeared before drifting back into a deep sleep. She struggled to wake up when her alarm clock went off, but somehow dragged herself to the bathroom. Half an hour later she was dressed and looking her usual well groomed self before setting off down to the restaurant to meet the others. They had another packed day of shopping, sightseeing, eating and drinking before all going to their separate rooms by ten thirty as they were all exhausted.

So on the last night, Gillian expected the same thing to happen again and it did. But there was a slight difference in that the sailor's face was clearer but he still wrapped his arms around his waist before slowly fading away. When he had completely disappeared she just lay in the dark with her eyes closed but unlike the previous two nights she was unable to get back to sleep. Her mind was working overtime. Imagine what the other two would say if she told them. They would probably laugh at her and say it was a dream. She opened her eyes to convince herself she was not being silly, she was definitely awake when she saw the sailor. Was he there to tell her something? His features were Chinese. Is that why he picked on her room? She had to admit that since her partner left her, she hadn't really felt as happy as she used to be. There was something else that kept her awake. Since she and Joe exchanged glances on Saturday, she couldn't get him off her mind. How could she think about someone who she didn't know? That was just silly. She realised that all of these thoughts were just ridiculous and maybe tiredness was just exacerbating her thoughts. She tried to clear her mind and eventually drifted off to sleep, with just an hour to go before the alarm went off.

Six months later, Gillian was helping her mother clear out her father's mothers house. Her grandmother had been in a nursing home for sometime but her house wasn't put up for sale until she passed away. Gillian was upstairs sorting out a cupboard in her gran's bedroom. She went through a box of papers, studying each one just to make sure she didn't throw anything away that was important. There were alot of paper cuttings, most of which she couldn't see any point in keepings so placed them on the recycling pile. One piece was very old, she opened it with care and noticed the headline;

Seaman dies on the Albert Dock

Gillian read the article and noticed the last name of the seaman had the same name as her family. She took the paper clipping over to the window where it was lighter and read the full article. The Chinese seaman had died tragically unloading bales of cotton. One fell on him and knocked him straight into the water. He drowned before anyone could get to him. He had a big funeral which included many other Chinese seamen and their families.

Gillian went and sat on the bedroom chair to think about what she had read. So her experience whilst on her girls weekend, the image of what she thought was a sailor, may have been the seaman, a relative? 'Wow, this is all so strange,' she thought.

"Gill, love, how are you doing?" Her mum came into the room.

Gillian showed her mum the newspaper article. Her mum read it.

"I had heard that your father's great, great grandad had died in an accident, but no one has really talked about it, maybe because it was so long ago. Anyway, we really need to get going, we have to go to the tip on the way home before it closes."

Gillian folded up the article and popped it in her bag downstairs. She collected all the recycling and rubbish together with her mother and they both left.

Eventually, when Gillian went to bed that night at her flat, she thought of those nights at the hotel. Someone else was still on her mind since the weekend break, Joe, the man who they had just spent a few hours with. Also, the man she knew nothing about and didn't even have him as a friend on Facebook, because she had given up social media. She did her best to put Joe out of her mind and concentrate on the sightings during the night in room number ten at the hotel on the Albert Dock. Gillian decided she was going to go back again, on her own and see if she could request the same room again. She hadn't spoken with Pamela or Tina since returning, which was normal because they were all busy, but they all understood each other and they would soon be in touch again to arrange the annual weekend away.

The very next day, Gillian rang up the hotel and booked two nights and requested room ten stating how much she had loved the view from a previous stay. She was due to go the following month. She also made up her mind that she would open a new Facebook account and just add a few chosen friends; she now felt ready to look at friends' photos and stories. That evening Gillian set up the Facebook account and the first couple of friend's requests she sent were of course Tina and Pamela. They were both delighted she had come back on and both messaged with her, catching up and suggesting where they might meet for their next weekend away. Gillian wondered if their friends list were available to see. Tina's were private, but Pamela's wasn't. Gillian scrolled down until eventually she found Joe. Just as she was about to click on his profile, a message came through from Pamela.

Oh darling, I forgot to tell you, the guy we met on the ferry, Joe, sends occasional messages and always asks about you. Nice chap. Take care babe, I'm just off for a shower xxxxx

Gillian looked at his photos which were available to see. She debated whether to send him a friend's request but decided to send some to her other friend first. In the end she bottled out.

Several weeks later, Gillian walked around the Albert Dock enjoying the beautiful evening sunshine after arriving for her two night break. She hadn't mentioned going back to Liverpool to Tina and Pamela. They had many conversations about where the three of them would go next but Gillian wanted to keep her lone weekend break to herself. When she arrived back at the hotel, she used the room service to have an evening meal sent up to her hotel room. When she had finished, she sat in bed and read a book. It was still fairly early but she felt tired and drifted into a deep sleep until suddenly she woke up with a start. The outline of the man who looked like a sailor was what she was faced with when she opened her eyes. She watched until the man wrapped his arms around his waist and then slowly he faded away. Gillian pinched herself, and looked around the dark room, trying to convince herself that she was not dreaming and really was awake. Finally, she went back to sleep until woken by her phone alarm.

She dressed and went down to the restaurant, where she chose a croissant and some fruit for breakfast. She had picked up some leaflets from the reception area on the way so whilst eating she browsed through the leaflets, seeing if there was something that took her interest for her to visit. She read about the cultural aspects of the city, including the large Chinese community. It said that in the nineteenth century a large number of Chinese immigrants arrived due to a big company employing a large number of seamen. She also read about the hotel's history and it was built on the spot of the base where seamen worked. To her astonishment she read that It was the base where her father's great, great grandad had been killed. So this hotel stood on a place near to where he had lost his life. This was all so bizarre. This must be the ghost of him and he was trying to tell her something. She was totally convinced of that.

'Right' she thought. 'You only live once, I'm going to send Joe a Facebook friend's request.'

She did it immediately and within seconds, it was accepted. She was just finishing her croissant when a message came through.

Great to hear from you Gillian! How are you keeping? I hope you enjoyed the rest of that weekend with your friends.

I did thanks Joe, in fact so much I have come back on my own for some more this weekend.

Wow, that's great, I'm working shortly, but I'll finish about six. Would you like me to show you some sights after work?

Gillian tried to remain calm and not look too keen, because there may be nothing to be keen about. He was just being friendly.

If you can spare the time, that would be lovely, thank you.

They arranged to meet at six thirty in the bar of her hotel. Gillian continued to sit over her coffee for quite a while, thinking over the past three years since her partner left. She had more or less not really lived, cut herself off from many people she knew and just kept a few close pals. She realised that she needed to start living properly again. It was no use thinking that Joe would be anything other than a friendly guy who was keen to talk about his home city, but thinking of him had made her try to heal the wound she had been left with since her partner had gone. It had made her realise she could go on and have another relationship and perhaps find happiness again.

Eventually, Gillian left the table, went to her room to freshen up, then set off sightseeing.

She returned to the hotel late afternoon, had a shower and laid on the bed in her dressing gown reading her book. She then got herself ready. She brushed her long shiny, black hair which had dried naturally whilst she read. She applied a little mascara, blusher and lip gloss. Her loose blouse flowed over her neat trousers and comfy shoes. She grabbed her tiny handbag and jacket before making her way down to the bar. She ordered herself a coffee whilst she waited for Joe.

Joe walked into the bar, spot on six thirty. He looked around and saw Gilian sipping her coffee. She stood up when she saw him walking towards her. She thought how dashing he looked in smart chino trousers and a casual checked shirt. They both sat down and chatted immediately as if they had known each other for years. After about twenty minutes, Gillian turned to Joe.

"How about we get you a drink?"

He laughed and nipped to the bar. He came back with a beer and two restaurant menus.

"I've not eaten so we could have a meal before we go out?"

The pair never did go out to sightsee, they just chatted and chatted.

It turned out that Joe was a skipper on one of the boats at the docks. For some reason, Gillian, knowing he worked long hours, thought he had a Chinese restaurant like her father. Joe laughed at that saying he couldn't even cook.

At midnight, a happy but tired Gillian was getting ready for bed, in the knowledge that she would spend the next day with Joe, who had a day off. She hadn't told anyone about her ghostly sightings in room ten, which had now happened on four occasions. It was something she wanted to keep to herself. In her mind, the gestures of the sailor almost hugging himself was a message to her. That she could find love and peace again.

She fell into a contented sleep, until she woke up again with a start. In the darkness she saw the image of the sailor, she sat up, pulling the sheet up to her chin. This time, he lifted up his arms and held them outstretched in front of him, his hands almost beckoning her…then he just faded away.

Gillian lay back on the pillows. She smiled as she shut her eyes and thought of what she had just seen. Some things happen for a reason.

She was sure he was telling her, it was fine to move on and break free from the past.

'Thank you, great, great, great grandad for guiding me. I know it was you.'

She had a feeling that her and Joe were meant to be. She hoped that, despite the little bit they knew about each other, the miles between their homes, there was a bond between them that meant they could overcome any obstacles.

Then she thought about Tina and Pamela. She hoped she would have something exciting to tell them on their next…Girlie Weekend!!

The Sounds of Healing

—◊◊—

VANESSA WENT UPSTAIRS to find some old family photos. There was a big cabinet in the spare bedroom with baskets of old photos on the shelves along with stacks of photo albums. She sighed when she pulled out a basket and thought, 'How much easier it is these days to have your pictures on your phone. What am I going to do with all these photos?' Mind you, when she showed pictures to older people on her phone, they complained about the small screen and how they preferred looking at "proper" photos. You can't please everyone.

She sifted through the basket which she thought contained the photos she was looking for. As she flicked through, occasionally pulling the odd one out and cringing at ones of herself, she came across an old faded photograph of a band she went to see many years ago. She carried the photo over to the spare bed, sat down and studied it. Memories came flooding back. The photo had been signed by the band members but the signatures were barely legible, they had faded over time.

The photo reminded her of growing up without her beloved mother. She was ten and a half years old when her mother suddenly died. It was a terrible shock, so sudden, leaving both her and her older sister with their lives turned upside down. It wasn't as if she had been ill for long and back then no one really told them anything. Her mum went into hospital and never came out. As children, they were always sent up to their rooms if adults wanted to talk privately and when it was the day of the funeral they were sent to relatives. Somehow life carried on. When Vanessa reached the age of twelve, her elder sister who was then seventeen, went off to France to stay with a pen friend. She ended up finding a job and staying there. Vanessa was lost without her and often shut herself in her room and sobbed. She had some nice, caring friends but as she had no mother, she would often just walk around and knock on friends doors to see if they would come out. This did not always make her very popular with some of her friends' parents and she remembered being told to go away by one of them.

Now, as she looked back, it was probably a bit mean because it wasn't her fault that her family were not like all the others. Most of her friends lived with their mums and dads. There were fewer divorces and couples tended to marry, not 'live in sin' as it was called back then. She had one other friend who lived just with her dad. Maybe it would have been different now? There was no counselling and no sympathy in those days, you just had to get on with it.

She didn't see that much of her dad, he went to work, then often went out with friends when he finished. Over the years, she didn't bother much with school and spent holidays with her late mum's mother, Grandma Mary in Bristol. For the first few years, Grandma Mary was still working part time, cleaning in an office nearby. This meant Vanessa spent that time on her own. She would often go out and wander around the shops in Bristol. Occasionally, she enjoyed her own company, just walking around in her own world, but that was probably because she knew she would go back to Grandma Mary and not an empty home. When she got a bit older, she felt less 'lonely' even though she missed her mum and sister terribly.

Back to the present and still sitting on the spare room bed, Vanessa gazed at the photo of the band 'Gonzalez'. She had loved music in her teen years although still haunted by the very thought of hearing 'Tie a Yellow Ribbon Round the Ole Oak Tree' sung by Tony Orlando and Dawn. It was number one in the pop charts for months and it was during that time her mother had suddenly passed away. What a strange thing to remember. Her mother's death was on Easter Saturday. The doctor came round to visit her family just a couple of hours after they had received the dreadful news on that awful day and gave her a drink of tea containing a shot of whisky. Why would a doctor put whisky in a ten year olds tea? Maybe that's what they did then.

Vanessa smiled to herself then at the thought of whisky! That's probably why she has not touched the stuff since, or any other spirits either. She actually started laughing to herself. Maybe if all ten year olds were given whisky in their cup of tea, it might put them off strong spirits forever! Nowadays, she couldn't even bear to look at a bottle of whisky and would probably throw up at the smell of it. Disgusting stuff!

Her thoughts then turned to her beautiful Grandma Mary, who had passed away when she was eighty two, having lost both her daughter and husband far too early. Grandma Mary lived in a terraced house in the heart of Bristol. Vanessa loved staying with her. It was good for both of them and they spent hours talking about the good times they had spent with Vanessa's mother. It brought them so close together. Grandma Mary was at the time considered to be a 'very modern grandma.' She understood Vanessa's needs as she was growing up and they could talk about anything. Vanessa closed her eyes, picturing Grandma Mary's beautiful face.

"Mum, what are you doing?"

Vanessa nearly fell off the bed.

"Goodness, you made me jump, Ben!"

Ben was Vanessa's younger son who still lived at home and was studying for his Masters Degree at a local university.

"I was hoping to find what I was looking for before you got back," she laughed.

"Why?"

"Because my cousin's son was in some photos with you when you were kids. We haven't seen him since but he is coming to the family reunion in Gloucester that we are going to in a few weeks, so I wanted to find the photos of you both to take, along with a few others."

"I see mum, so you just want to embarrass us both!" Ben laughed.

"Well, we can see if you have both changed! Don't worry I will take some of your sister when she was little too!"

"What's that photo of an old fashioned looking band, you've got there?" Ben asked.

"Just a group I liked when I was young, I was young once you know!"

Ben laughed and walked off to his bedroom. 'What a great lad he is,' she thought. 'I have been well and truly blessed with my family.'

Vanessa decided to give up the search for photos and make a start on preparing some food now Ben was home.

She went downstairs into the kitchen. She would generally put on the small TV in the corner whilst she prepared the tea. She liked 'The Chase' and would see how many questions she could get right, which was generally no more than two at the most during the whole programme.

Tonight, she decided to put on her bluetooth speaker and find a Gonzalez song to listen to whilst she prepared the risotto. On her phone she found the Gonzalez hit which was probably their most well known one and put it on. As she chopped the onions she sang along.

"I haven't stopped dancing yet…"

Ben came into the kitchen with his hands over his ears and turned down the speaker.

"Mum, what is this song? If you must put your speaker on when I'm here, let's listen to something a bit more up to date!" He teased her.

He scrolled down her phone which was on the kitchen table and put on a modern tune. Vanessa playfully ruffled his already unruly hair.

A week later, Vanessa decided to go on another photo search. The family reunion was looming and she wanted to put the photos in a small photo album that would fit in her handbag. She went into the spare room again and pulled out the basket. The photo of Gonzalez was sitting on the top. She went back downstairs and fetched her speaker from the kitchen. She decided to try again and play the music whilst Ben was not around! 'I Haven't Stopped Dancing Yet' played loudly from her speaker.

She thought back to how much she had played that record, over and over again. Grandma Mary used to hear Vanessa playing her music in her bedroom on her small record player that she had bought for her. She had known how much music had meant to Vanessa. She realised that music was a therapy for her granddaughter helping to ease the sadness and loneliness she sensed Vanessa was going through.

Vanessa felt herself welling up thinking about Grandma Mary. She was such an incredible woman. When she reflected about those times, she wondered why she hadn't just gone and lived with her after her sister left home. If she had, then maybe she wouldn't have felt so desolate during those years. It would have probably been easier for her father too. He had been at a loss at times with his teenage daughter and her unpredictable moods, particularly as he was busy with his job and friends.

Grandma Mary could read Vanessa like a book. The summer that Vanessa finished school for good, Grandma Mary invited Vanessa and her best friend to stay for a couple of weeks. Vanessa was so excited to take Sharon with her. They were now old enough to take the train to Bristol Templemead Station where Grandma Mary would meet them. When they arrived Grandma Mary was on the platform and greeted them both with open arms. The three of them linked arms and set off on the short walk to her home. Grandma Mary had made a delicious cottage pie for them all for tea. Once they had all eaten she made an announcement.

"Vanessa, I know you love Gonzalez, you are always playing their album so I've got a pair of tickets for you and Sharon to see them. I saw a poster when I was out shopping advertising the event. I thought to myself, I know my Vanessa and Sharon would love to go. It's in two days' time."

Vanessa leapt off the chair and hugged her grandma. Sharon then got up and hugged them both.

Vanessa had tears streaming down her face as she reminisced

on that evening. She put the song on replay as she thought of the fabulous evening that she had with Sharon. They danced all night to the music and eventually after hanging around at the end, Vanessa got her album cover signed by some of the band members. Grandma Mary had even walked from her home to meet them both at the end. The three of them walked back to Grandma's home, both girls excitedly relaying the evening's events to a delighted Grandma Mary. They arrived back just before midnight.

"Mum, have you got that old music on again?" Ben shouted to Vanessa as he walked into the spare room making her jump again. "Haven't you sorted out the photos yet?"

Vanessa looked at the basket, she hadn't even taken one photo out of it.

"Mum, are you okay?" Ben looked concerned as he studied Vanessa's red eyes.

"Yes love. I was just thinking of Grandma Mary. It's a shame you can't remember her, she was a brilliant grandma. Let's go and get some tea."

Vanessa and Ben went downstairs. They both had a mug of coffee before she went over to the work surface to prepare the evening meal.

"You know Ben, Grandma really understood me, I don't know how I would have survived those teenage years without her."

Ben grinned at his mum.

"I'm glad I have you mum, you understand me...well sometimes you do!"

Vanessa put her knife down from peeling potatoes, turned around to Ben, still sitting at the kitchen table and smiled at him.

Finally, the day of the family reunion arrived. Vanessa had eventually managed to get her small family photo album ready and it fitted perfectly in her handbag. The reunion had been organised by one of Grandma Mary's sisters' daughters, called Melanie. Vanessa didn't know Melanie very well, having only seen her on rare occasions and that was another reason why she had fished out some old photos. In fact, she only expected to know about half the people there and some she hadn't seen since she was a child. Because her mother had died when she was so young, she had only really kept in touch with her grandma after that. Her father had never bothered with any of the relations on her mothers side, except for Grandma Mary, but that was only for a few years, when he dropped Vanessa off until she was old enough to get to Bristol by train.

The reunion was held in Melanie's back garden and fortunately the weather was looking to stay fine and dry all day.

Once they arrived, Melanie greeted them and led them through the dining room where there was a beautiful table of food, with another table full of glasses and drinks. The patio doors were open and the garden was full of people. They spent the first half an hour catching up with the few relatives that Vanessa recognised. By lunchtime, the party was in full swing with everyone helping themselves to the buffet and drinks. By then, Vanessa's family were all mingling so Melanie came and sat next to Vanessa who was just finishing off her bowl of strawberries and cream.

"I'm so pleased you could come, Vanessa. I know you had a difficult time after your mum died. I'm so glad you had Auntie Mary to look after you."

"I don't know where I would have been without my lovely Grandma Mary." Vanessa replied.

Vanessa brought out her mini photo album from her handbag and Melanie and Vanessa reminisced on the couple of pictures of them together, with Vanessa, just a young child and Melanie slightly older. Vanessa had already introduced Melanie to her husband and children when they arrived but proudly showed her some earlier pictures of her family.

"You know what Vanessa," Melanie said. "Auntie Mary worked so hard to help you because you were in a bad place and she understood you. She knew how much music played such a big part in your grieving and healing process. I can remember her looking around the shops to get you a suitable record player. She was so pleased when she found the right one. She also knew how much you loved the record by Gonzalez."

Vanessa was astounded by what Melanie was saying, because she wasn't aware that any other relatives knew much about her. Melanie carried on talking about memories of her auntie and Vanessa's grandma as they browsed through the photo album together.

"I'm just going to fetch something," Melanie said to Vanessa. She returned with an envelope. Vanessa opened it and pulled out a photo. It was a black and white photo of a man who looked familiar. On the reverse side was a message.

My best wishes to you Vanessa. I'm glad the band was able to help with making your life more bearable all those years ago. Take care. Love and best wishes Lenny xxx

Vanessa looked at the photo again. It was the lead singer of Gonzalez, the band that along with Grandma Mary and Sharon helped her to get through those traumatic years.

"I tracked him down!" Melanie laughed.

Vanessa hugged Melanie. She would treasure it forever. She would also show it to her family when they got home, when she felt ready to.

Vanessa couldn't get to sleep that night. She just lay in bed thinking, her husband fast asleep next to her. They had all had such a great time. Ben had found her cousin's son and complained when Vanessa brought out the photo album containing two pictures of them together! She had met so many relatives that she would have probably had more contact with, had her mother not passed away. But, it was not too late and another family reunion was planned for the following year. Her children would keep in touch with the relatives they had met up with on social media. Vanessa said a silent prayer for Grandma Mary. In those days, there may have been no sympathy, empathy or counselling when such a traumatic event happened but thanks to Grandma Mary and of course Gonzalez and their album 'Shipwrecked' she had come out the other side.

"I haven't stopped dancing yet……" Vanessa smiled, closed her eyes and slept.

A subject close to the hearts of my old school friend Vanessa Lander and myself.

Lenny Zakatek – Lead singer of Gonzalez
Thank you for the music!

The Tales of the Over 55's Day Centre

Part 1 – Millennium Surprises!

—⚏—

EDNA SAT AT the table, hands cupped around her mug of coffee. She was wracking her brains trying to think of some way to celebrate the turn of the century. It was October 1999. Edna was a regular volunteer at her local day centre. She had somehow stumbled into the role of event organiser, due to the charity unable to fund a 'paid' one. She was brought out of her thoughts by two of the regular visitors to the centre. Joyce and her sister Margaret were two lively ladies who loved the centre. They attended two days a week, enjoyed the socialising, the three course home cooked lunches and carpet bowls. They were always laughing, their laughter was infectious. If anyone came to the centre feeling depressed, it wouldn't be long before Joyce and Margaret cheered them up. Joyce always called her sister 'Maggie.'

"Look Maggie, there's Edna sitting over there, let's go and see how she is."

Edna's eyes lit up when the jovial pair sat down opposite her. "Hello both, how are you doing?"

The three of them 'put the world to rights' until the place began to fill up as people flocked in for their lunch and afternoon activities. The dining room was a large cheery room. The tables were decorated with checked tablecloths with small vases containing a little posy of fresh flowers situated in the middle of each one. Each table was surrounded by comfortable chairs, with arms on, so that those who might have difficulty with sitting to standing, could use them to assist. Edna joined some of the other volunteers, helping them with serving out the three course lunch. The atmosphere was, as usual, happy and noisy as the 'young at heart' folk enjoyed the food. Soon after lunch, many of the visitors made their way to the adjoining coffee bar area, where they sat on relaxing, comfortable arm chairs to enjoy their after lunch coffee.

Joyce and Margaret remained at the dinner table and when Edna had finished clearing up with the other helpers, she joined them bringing her coffee with her.

"You didn't have anything to eat, Edna?" Joyce said.

"No, lovey, I don't eat anything at lunchtime normally, I will eat later at home. I don't eat much these days," she laughed. "Just enough to keep going, not like I used to eat in my younger days!" The three of them laughed and then Joyce spoke.

"I've got an idea, Edna."

Margaret raised her eyebrows.

"What's up with you Maggie?" Joyce grinned at her sister. "I do have ideas occasionally you know!"

"I know, that's what worries me. They are generally rude!"

Joyce playfully smacked Margaret's arm.

"No, I wouldn't say anything rude to Edna."

Margaret kept her fingers crossed but didn't hold out much hope.

"When we were chatting earlier Edna, you mentioned you wanted to do a fundraising event to celebrate the New Year and something special as it's the Millennium, not the usual rummage sale or coffee morning."

Margaret waited with baited breath, dreading what would come out of Joyce's mouth.

"What about a fashion show?"

Margaret sighed with relief. 'That sounds fairly good, so far,' she thought.

Joyce carried on.

"The volunteers can model the clothes, including swimwear."

Margaret held her breath, dreading what was coming next.

"The clothes will be a selection from the twentieth century. We can sell tickets and the cat walk can be down the centre of the dining room. The tables can be moved and we can put chairs either side of the catwalk. Also, we can be saucy and wear low cut tops, mini skirts and bikinis!!"

Margaret was eighty two and the thought of walking down the catwalk in swimwear made her rock in her chair laughing. She just couldn't stop, Joyce joined in and because their laughter was so infectious, Edna began chuckling. Before long all three of them were laughing hysterically at the thought of them modelling down the catwalk. Everytime one of them went to say something, they couldn't get the words out for laughing. Margaret stood up and pulled her dress up to mini skirt height and did a twirl. Joyce then unbuttoned the top three buttons of her lacy cream blouse, stood up, placed her hands on her hips, pushed her chest out, and pouted.

A male volunteer walked past their table, looked at Joyce and hurried on by.

By then the three of them were almost crying with laughter, having seen the look on the volunteer's face.

Edna was beginning to think this could actually be a great idea because not only would it raise money by way of ticket sales, raffle and refreshment sales, it would be fun.

"Joyce, you are on!" she said. "We need to ask the other volunteers if they will model."

Edna smiled all the way home. She was seventy six years old and had been a widow for some years. The centre provided a bus which picked up the visitors from their homes and took them to the centre, then dropped them home later in the afternoon. It was very busy so the bus made several trips back and forth each day. Edna was one of several volunteers and although she was older than some of the visitors, she was able to make her way to and from the centre on foot with the assistance of her shopping trolley.

Over the next few months, Edna kept an eye on what clothes were being donated to the charity shop which was situated at the front of the day centre. She was looking for suitable items to wear for The Twentieth Century Millenium Fashion Show. That was the name the volunteers had chosen for the event. The clothes were to be washed afterwards and put back in the charity shop after the show.

The three ladies 'roped' three other volunteers and one visitor to model at the fashion show. They were all game for a laugh including the one male volunteer who was seventy eight years old. The Manager of the centre would be compere for the afternoon. The small fashion show 'committee' of eight including the Manager held regular meetings to discuss the event and it was decided to hold it on a Wednesday afternoon two weeks before Christmas. The centre was closed at various times around

Christmas and the New Year so they thought it would be a fun event to have at the start of the festive season.

By mid November, Edna had collected several bags of clothing and at the weekly meeting she put all the items out on a table so the group could choose what clothes they would wear to model. They were also going to adapt some clothes to fit in with different decades. One of the volunteers was very clever at dressmaking. It was a very busy meeting. They also agreed that two clothes changes would be enough for each model.

That afternoon meeting was full of laughs as they chose what they were each going to wear. Joyce had made up her mind she was going to be a 'sixties' girl, so she picked up a skirt and held it against herself. It was far too long so she hoisted it up to try and make it a mini skirt, which was a sixties fashion item. The dressmaker volunteer laughed.

"Here Joyce, pop it on over your dress, I've got my pins so I will tack it up," she said.

"You better tack it up short, I want my sexy pins showing!" Joyce chuckled.

Margaret pulled a face at Joyce.

"It was me, your older sister who had the sexy pins in the sixties, not you! You had big boobs, remember! ...mind you where did they go?"

Joyce pretended to be cross with her sister, then bent over to her handbag, opened it up and pulled out two balls of cotton wool.

"These, my dear sister, are to be stuffed down my bra, because the boobs did go...downwards."

By then they were all laughing, even the male volunteer who was bemused by the two sisters' antics.

A week after the lively fun filled meeting disaster struck. Margaret was taken ill and had to stay at home to recover. Joyce carried on with her visits to the centre and the fashion show meetings but really missed her sister being with her. She just lived in hope that Margaret would be able to take part but if she couldn't, she was able to sit and watch it.

Margaret's health did improve but a week before the fashion show, Margaret's daughter Carol rang Joyce.

"Joyce love, I don't think mum will be well enough to take part in the fashion show, but I will bring her to watch. I know she will be disappointed but the main thing is that she will be there."

Joyce was upset, but as Carol had said Margaret would be there to watch. It will do her good.

The big day arrived. It was a beautiful sunny, cold and crisp morning. The sky was blue and clear, full of vapour trails from the planes flying above. Edna was happily looking at them as she walked to the centre. Her trolley was full of her outfits for her catwalk debut. She reflected as she walked. They had all put a lot of hard work and effort into this day. The raffle prizes had been set out the day before. Cake donations had been coming in to go with the hot drinks, to be served at the interval. But best of all, the event had been a sell out and by two o'clock the place would be full. Edna felt cheerful, it was going to be a great day, she just knew it would be.

At one thirty the 'models' were in their dressing rooms, a side room for the ladies and the men's toilets for the one male model. Ray had taken many items home to try on but had not disclosed to the others what he would be wearing. The compere, the Centre Manager was going to introduce him by the decade his outfits represented.

The ladies were laughing together as usual. Joyce had her mini skirt and blouse on, with her 'cotton wool' chest. She was parading around the room practising her catwalk moves. She was so pleased that her beloved sister, Margaret, could come and watch.

Margaret, her daughter Carol and Joyce's daughter Allyson had all taken their seats, the very best seats right at the front.

By a quarter to two, the centre was buzzing. It was such a wonderful atmosphere. The centre was full of beautiful Christmas decorations. There was a real Christmas tree set in the corner and Christmas music playing softly in the background.

At two o'clock The Twentieth Century Millenium Fashion Show began.

The Manager welcomed everyone and introduced the first 'model'. Several of the models representing the different decades paraded down the catwalk to cheers and clapping. Joyce's turn came. She walked down the catwalk slowly in her sixties outfit. Her confidence in impersonating young catwalk models brought the house down. She was in her element and so was Margaret who was clapping and cheering her. Joyce reached the end of the catwalk, did a twirl and pulled out a handkerchief from her 'low cut' blouse and waved it in the air to the music. After Joyce's amazing performance, it was time for refreshments during the interval and the sale of the raffle tickets. The raffle was to be drawn at the end. Joyce went to sit with Margaret and their daughters for a few minutes before returning to the dressing room.

Some forty five minutes later, the second half began. The first 'model' was the gentleman volunteer Ray, who scrubbed up very well in his 'twenties' suit and hat. He was also to be 'modelling' again as the last act of the show. Edna was the next 'model'. She did a gentle stroll down the catwalk in a beautiful flowing outfit. She looked amazing. It soon came round for Joyce's turn again. People could not believe their eyes when Joyce walked down the catwalk dressed like a cat woman complete with eye mask and ears. She purred and wiggled her way down to the end. She was clearly in her element and enjoying the moment. Finally, Ray burst onto the catwalk dressed in fifties beachwear to everyone's surprise! He danced down the catwalk to the music and received a standing ovation. He loved every minute as did the audience.

It finally came to an end, far too soon. The clapping just didn't seem to stop. The Manager stood with the microphone waiting for the clapping to die down.

"Thank you so much everyone, that is the end of the show…"

"Oh no it's not!" a voice shouted from the audience.

Everyone looked around.

Margaret stood up, she walked over to the start of the catwalk. She took her cardigan off, twirled it around and threw it out to the audience. Carol stood up, hands on her hips, ready to go and grab her mother. She caught Joyce's eye and they both laughed. There was no stopping Margaret, she would always do what she wanted to do. Carol sat down and watched her lovely mum do what she had obviously set out to do.

Margaret then unbuttoned her dress, took it off, threw it to Carol and began to gently dance her way down the catwalk …in her swim wear! Her bathing costume was put on over her 'Nora Batty' style, thick brown tights and on her feet she had a pair of furry zip up boots!

She reached the bottom of the catwalk, smiling. Carol cheered and clapped, Edna smiled broadly and clapped, infact, the whole audience cheered and whistled.

Joyce stood up and shouted.

"Look at your pins Maggie, They still look great!"

What an amazing finale to a fabulous event.

Edna's daughter Anne, who had come to watch the show, stood up after the raffle had been drawn and thanked her mum and the volunteers for their fabulous show, before taking a happy but exhausted Edna home.

As they left the centre, arm in arm to walk to Anne's car, a few flakes of snow had started to fall from the dark skies. It was as if the snow had held off long enough for them to make sure everyone could get to the centre for the most amazing afternoon. An afternoon which Edna and her friends had worked so hard to make a success and raise a vast amount of money to help keep the essential service going.

The snowflakes were settling on the pavement and glistening in the light shining down from the streetlights.

Edna looked up at the dark sky and smiled.

Merry Christmas, Happy New Year and a Happy New Century to everyone!

Remembering two comical ladies- Margaret and Joyce!

Also, Thanking Edna 98, for her ongoing charity work and kind heart.

Part 2 – It's Just Because I Care.

—◊—

EDNA WALKED INTO the day centre pushing her faithful shopping trolley through the sliding doors.

"Morning all." she shouted to two of the other volunteers who were standing chatting together in the dining room.

"Morning Edna, love," one of them responded. The other waved and smiled.

It was a beautiful, sunny, Spring morning. Edna, as usual, had walked the short distance from her home to the centre, taking time to pop into the supermarket and chat to some of the locals she knew. Whilst walking, her thoughts had been about one of the centre visitors called Milly. Milly had been coming to the centre for a couple of years. She was a very private lady and didn't join in with any of the social activities but usually interacted with the others who sat with her in the dining room. Milly came to the centre every day that it was open, which was Monday to Friday, except Bank Holidays. When she first started coming, Edna had been allocated the job of calling for her on her first day because she lived nearby. Milly had invited her in whilst she fetched her bag and it was an immaculate terraced house.

Recently, Edna was getting concerned about Milly. She assumed Milly had no immediate family and in recent months had been quite withdrawn and was looking a bit unkempt. Although it pained Edna to even think it, Milly also did have an unpleasant smell about her. One of the more outspoken volunteers was heard to have commented on the smell.

The year was 2002 and Edna, who was now in her late seventies, usually helped out most weekdays at the centre, saving the weekdays to catch up at home and see her family. Her daughter, Anne knew that her mother worried about the well being of others and had gently suggested she mustn't spend too much time dwelling on other people. Anne did her best to make sure that Edna went out on the weekends and spent time with younger people. Anne had a lot of friends and she would often arrange to meet one or two at a coffee shop on a Saturday morning. She would take Edna along so she could mix with younger people. Edna enjoyed those times, listening to their holiday tales and their laughter.

Once Edna had chatted with the two other volunteers in the dining room, she went to park her shopping trolley in its usual place then fetched the neatly ironed tablecloths from the store cupboard. She put a tablecloth on each table then sorted out the vases containing a couple of fresh flowers out and placed them and the salt and pepper pots on each table. There was a bit of time before the mini bus dropped off the passengers from its first pick up at the centre so she went to the coffee bar, made a hot drink then sat on one of the comfortable chairs in the coffee bar area.

She shut her eyes, not with the intention of going to sleep but just relaxing in the sunlight streaming through the window. She opened her eyes when she was aware of a shadow near her.

She looked up and saw Doctor Victor just about to sit down opposite her. Victor had been the local Doctor in the small town where they lived many years previously. He began coming to the centre after his wife of fifty years passed away suddenly. He allowed the volunteers just to call him Vic when he turned up each day for his lunch. As a Doctor, Vic had been very caring and quite friendly, but in recent years, he behaved like he had lost his sense of purpose. It was as though he attended the centre for a meal each day to survive and had little interest in much else.

"Hello Vic," Edna smiled at him.

He nodded back at her and grunted.

"Can I help you with anything? There's a popular men's group here on a Friday afternoon, they play cards."

Vic glared at her.

"No thanks," he mumbled.

Edna gave up with him, so she stood up and made her way to the dining room ready to meet the other guests. She looked towards the door to the dining room where some of the other visitors were walking in having come off the first bus pick up. She then noticed Gerry sitting at one of the tables reading some documents. Edna thoroughly disliked Gerry. Gerry had taken over as Centre Manager after Diane had left. They had all loved Diane and were very sorry to see her go. Edna thought back to Christmas just before the Millennium year when they had the wonderful fashion show, which had brought in so much money to help with the running costs. Diane had left not long after to be replaced by Gerry. Gerry was a very difficult man and his only strong point was that he spent most of his working day hidden in his office. He had put a stop to Edna's fundraising efforts, therefore the fashion show was never allowed to be repeated. All Edna had been able to do during the past couple of years was to sell her craft items on a stall at events he organised. In the last couple of years since he took over, none of his events had been as well turned out and as much fun as that very last event Edna arranged.

'I wonder why Gerry had decided to come out of his hideaway?' Edna thought to herself. 'Hope he goes back pretty soon and stays there.'

The dinner tables began to fill up and Edna reverted back to her usual cheerful self and greeted people. Once most people were seated and chatting noisily away to each other, Edna went over to talk to Milly, sitting alone on a table set out for four. Milly did not want to converse with Edna, so she gave up trying and went to help the other volunteers with delivering the meals to the tables. Edna did notice the unpleasant smell whilst going up to Milly and wondered if that's why others were now not sitting with her.

Edna set off for home during the middle of the afternoon once she had helped clear up after lunch. She would have usually remained for a while longer and joined in with the armchair exercises, but today she felt down. She pushed her trolley through the streets which were quite busy with people shopping. She got to where McDonalds was situated and crossed over at the traffic lights for the final part of her journey. 'It wasn't a great day.' she thought. 'I was only trying my best to be friendly, but then there was that awful Gerry. What is he up to?' Gerry had waited for a man with a briefcase to arrive, then once they had picked up a cup of tea each, disappeared into Gerry's office.

All evening, Edna felt upset. She wished Diane was still the Manager. Diane was a lovely woman, liked by everyone and treated everyone with utmost respect. Diane's mother lived in Scotland and when she was diagnosed with Dementia, Diane wouldn't hear of her going into a home, so as she had no family, Diane left her job and went to stay with her mother. That was now two and a half years ago and Gerry had taken her job. Edna did not normally dislike anyone, but she did Gerry. He was the total opposite to Diane. He ruined everything that Diane had built up. The only reason that Edna continued to volunteer was because she loved the other volunteers and the visitors who attended the centre. Thankfully, Gerry kept out the way and she rarely saw him. Edna also felt sad about Vic being so abrupt and Milly not wanting to talk. When she went to bed, the events of that day played on her mind. She knew she must not mention this to her daughter Anne because she would want her to stop going. 'No, I must get over this, tomorrow is another day,' she thought before she eventually went to sleep.

The following week Edna noticed again that Milly was sitting on her own and when she left which was straight after she had finished the dessert, Edna noticed that she had left her purse on the table. She said to one of the other volunteers that she would drop Milly's purse to her on the way home. When she left the centre, she only had to make a short detour to Milly's home. She put the purse inside her shopping trolley. When she arrived at Milly's she noticed the once immaculate house looked neglected from the outside. She knocked on the door and handed Milly the purse. The door opened straight into the lounge and Edna noticed straightaway that the place looked a total mess, completely different to the time a few years ago when Edna had walked with Milly to the centre on her first day there.

"There you are lovey, you left it on the table."

"Thank you for bringing it round," Milly quickly closed the door, leaving Edna standing there. Edna arranged her shopping trolley and set off home. She walked past the local park where she noticed Doctor Victor sitting on a seat. He had his head in his hands. She walked as quickly as she was able towards her home.

The next day, a concerned Edna decided to have a word with Gerry about Milly and Doctor Victor. She didn't want to but as he was the Manager she had no choice. She knocked on his office door and when he invited her in, she told him how worried she was about Doctor Victor and Milly.

"Edna, we are just here to provide a service, there's nothing we can do about their problems, if indeed they have problems, or you just think they do," Gerry said to Edna, without looking at her, his face still looking down at his notepad. Edna just thanked him for sparing his time to help her and hurriedly left his office. She was upset by his attitude but not really surprised.

One Saturday morning a few weeks later, Edna's daughter Anne picked Edna up and took her to the coffee shop to have drinks with three of her friends. Edna always looked forward to the coffee mornings. Anne's friend's were such fun and she loved listening to the banter between them all. She sat there, quietly taking it all in and pleased her daughter had such lovely, caring friends.

Anne and her friends picked up their drinks and pastries from the counter. Anne also bought Edna a coffee and a croissant and took it over to Edna who had gone straight to a table when they entered the cafe. Tina sat next to Edna.

"How are you Edna?" Tina enquired.

"I'm fine darling, how are you?" The two of them exchanged further pleasantries for the next few minutes. The ladies all enjoyed a lively, fun morning. Tina turned to Anne just as they were getting ready to leave.

"I love your mum Anne, can I share her with you!" Tina joked.

"Course you can!" Anne laughed back, but then on a serious note she turned to Tina.

"You haven't made up with your mum then Tina?"

Anne wasn't sure what the situation was with Tina and her mother, only that Tina had fallen out with her well over twenty years ago around the time that Anne and Tina met, when they both started working together. It was not normally a subject which they talked about when they met up.

"No, I will never forget what she did. I don't even think of her as 'Mum', she is just Milly, a person who did a terrible thing. Luckily, I have never bumped into her nor that Doctor. I could not believe what I saw when I walked in on them all those years ago. I know mum was a widow but Doctor Victor was married and his wife was such a lovely popular lady."

Somehow, Edna managed to keep herself composed despite the shock statement. Of course, she had not mentioned any of her concerns to Anne, but she knew when she got home that she would have to tell Anne everything.

Tina put her arm around Edna, gave her a hug and they all left the coffee shop.

Anne took Edna home and said she would just come in for a few minutes before going home for lunch with her husband. Once inside, Edna told Anne everything about Milly and the Doctor and how uncaring Gerry was. Anne was amazed by what she heard, but also worried about Edna not getting any support from Gerry, particularly as she gave up so much time to help out at the centre. Anne knew this was not the time to discuss this with her mum, it would do on another day.

"You know what mum," Anne said to Edna. "I think I am going to have to tell Tina about how her mum is. Tina has always said she has no brothers and sisters so maybe it's time to forget the past and help her mum. I don't want to interfere in people's lives but she's such a good friend."

"Best of luck with that one, love. Maybe too much time has passed and they will never make it up, but then on the other hand, she is her flesh and blood." Edna replied.

Anne frowned at her mum.

"You know what mum, I wish you had told me all of this before. You work so hard at that centre and I want to know that you are valued and not worrying too much about the others. Mind you, nothing I say will change anything you do!"

Anne kissed her mum on the cheek, then left.

Edna flopped in a chair as soon as Anne had gone. She couldn't get over Tina suggesting that over twenty years ago Doctor Victor and Milly had an affair. She wondered if there had been a mistake? What had Tina seen? Maybe there was some logical explanation for what she saw? So many things going around Edna's mind. Edna's thoughts went back to Milly and Doctor Victor in the centre. She had no idea they even knew each other. She remembered once when the Doctor walked in for his lunch, she asked if he wanted to sit with Milly but he declined and went and sat somewhere else. That is fairly normal at the centre, so nothing unusual about that.

Eventually, Edna nodded off in her chair and woke up with a start at half past four. She decided she needed to stop fretting about other people and went to make herself a nice supper.

Over the following few weeks Edna did notice an improvement in Milly. She looked cleaner and smelt fresher and was a bit more sociable than she had been of late. She wondered and hoped that maybe Tina had made up with her mum, but she didn't know. All she knew was that Anne had told Tina that her mum knew Milly and how much she had worried about her.

One day the Chair of the Trustees turned up for lunch at the centre. He sat down for lunch with Gerry. Edna noticed Gerry's attitude was totally different that lunchtime, he was far more respectful to Edna and the other volunteers. Edna was annoyed because she realised that Gerry just put on an act when the very person who appointed him was there. She just wished that the Trustees saw the side of Gerry that the volunteers saw on a daily basis. She knew that there was no point in mentioning any negative comments to any of the Trustees because they wouldn't be believed.

Early afternoon one Friday after the lunch time rush, Edna saw Doctor Vic finishing off his coffee. Surprisingly, he had stayed a bit longer, most of the visitor's had gone home. There were no afternoon activities on Friday afternoons now, well not since Gerry had taken over. He liked to be locked up by three o'clock so he could get off for the weekend.

Edna decided to sit with Vic for a few minutes before he left. She kept her fingers crossed that he was in a slightly better mood since their last conversation.

"How are you Vic?" she asked as she pulled out a chair to sit down on.

"I'm fine thanks, Edna," he replied and to her amazement he actually smiled!

"That's good, it's nice to see you smile, you always look so sad."

Edna didn't mean to say that, she could have kicked herself and expected a rude or abrupt comment from Vic, but quite the opposite.

"I've realised that I can't change the past, what's done is done. I can't keep beating myself up about what I did in the past."

Edna couldn't believe what she was hearing and knew she would have to tread carefully.

"Was it that bad, Vic?"

"Yes because it was not as it seemed."

"What Vic?" Edna knew she was pushing her luck now.

"Many years ago I had an affair, and the lady who I had an affair with was disowned by her daughter and family, when we were caught together. She blamed me and has not spoken to me since. The trouble is, she attends this centre and I could see she was not bothering with herself, and I blame myself. I have noticed that in the last couple of weeks she looks a bit better, thank goodness. I know it was a long time ago but it's totally my fault for what she has gone through since. The worst thing was that my wife knew about her, but didn't mind. My wife didn't want me but refused to split up, so I wasn't actually upsetting my wife. I have caused such devastation to the lady and I have had to live with that."

Edna was feeling so sad listening to what Vic had said. Tina had been upset for Vic's wife but it looked as if it was Milly who had been affected and had her life ruined.

"Vic, is it Milly?" Edna asked him softly.

"Yes, I have to go now. I wish I could make her happy again, I've wrecked her life."

Vic got up and wished Edna a good weekend.

Gerry then appeared.

"Are we all packed up?" He shouted loudly so all the volunteers could hear him.

Edna looked at the wall clock. It was two thirty. She wasn't impressed. She decided to just fetch her trolley and set off home. Once she got out into the fresh air, she decided she was going to visit Milly, who had left the centre not long after one thirty. She didn't care if she was interfering or whatever it was called, she just knew that she couldn't see people unhappy, when they needn't be.

When she got to Milly's she knocked on the door and to her surprise it was opened by Tina.

"Edna! How lovely to see you. I'm so glad you told Anne about mum. Come in."

Edna went in and was so pleased to see the house had been cleaned up and Milly was sitting on the settee looking so much more relaxed.

"I've just come to tell you about Doctor Vic," Edna went straight in with it.

"He tells me that his wife wasn't interested in him and didn't care if he had a lady friend as long as they stayed married, so Tina love, she wasn't upset."

"Really Edna, I would like to think that, but what if he is just saying that because his wife is no longer here and can't defend herself?"

"I realise that, Tina. But I think he was telling the truth. Look Milly, you and Vic have looked so sad in recent times. You can't change the past, but you still have a life in front of you."

Milly smiled and Edna wished them all the best and set off home.

Several weeks later, Anne picked up Edna and took her for a Saturday morning coffee morning with her friends. Tina was there but this time she brought her own mother Milly. Tina hugged Edna before she sat down.

"We have something to tell you, mum and I are going for a meal tonight with Doctor Vic!" Tina said excitedly. Edna was so pleased, she prayed that this was going to be a happy ending and that her 'interfering' was only for the good. It was something that remained to be seen.

They all had a lively, chatty coffee morning. Milly looked so much better, almost like ten years had been taken off her. She couldn't stop looking at Tina. Edna decided that even if it had just brought mother and daughter back together, it was worth all her worry.

Two months later Edna had a 'new' job for the day. She put the special tablecloths on each of the tables in the dining room in the centre, She didn't just put a small posy of flowers in the middle, but a beautiful table arrangement on each one then sprinkled small silver horseshoes over the table. The dining room was transformed into a fabulous reception venue. She stood back after all the tables were ready and waited with the other volunteers for the arrival of… .

the newly weds …Doctor Victor and his lovely wife Milly!

Part 3 – A Bumpy Ride…
and a Happy Ending!

—⁓—

The group stood outside the day centre on the beautiful Saturday morning of July 5th 2003. They chatted happily whilst they waited for the coach, which was to take them to Sandringham in Norfolk, for the day. The day centre was closed at weekends so the car park was empty and the coach would be able to pull in.

The group of volunteers and visitors from the day centre had all agreed that they would have an away day. Gerry, the Manager of the centre had informed them that it was nothing to do with him and the centre would play no part in it. That is exactly what they expected of him. All the volunteers had now realised that Gerry was not the right person to manage a day centre which was also a registered charity. Edna, a day centre volunteer, had noticed that he behaved totally differently when in the presence of the Trustees, the very people who had employed him for the role. He had the ability to turn on the charm when they were around, but treated the volunteers with contempt. He was a complete opposite from the previous Manager, the lovely Diane who had left to look after her mother.

One of the volunteers insisted on organising the day trip with everyone assembling in the car park ready for an eight thirty getaway. Edna was concerned as to whether it would go smoothly because the volunteer then allocated the organising of it to her daughter. Edna knew the daughter and was aware that she was probably what you would describe as 'scatty' although very well meaning. Edna thought of the difference between her and her own daughter Anne, who was a very efficient lady. If Anne had organised it, there would be no hitches because she believed in attention to detail. Anyway, she couldn't keep asking Anne to do anymore, she did enough.

"Edna, the coach is here," Edna's friend Joan grabbed her arm, interrupting her thoughts.

Edna smiled at Joan. Joan was a great friend and she was so pleased to be spending the day with her. They both joined the queue to get on to the coach, whilst the coach driver put the array of four wheeled walkers and shopping trolleys into the luggage hold.

They set off on time when everyone was settled. Edna and Joan sat fairly near the front. The coach driver was not the friendliest, which was a shame as on previous coach trips a friendly coach driver could make the trip a lot more fun. Edna did note that the organiser had not used their usual coach company, where the drivers were knowledgeable and friendly. She recalled one coach driver chatting to the passengers over the loudspeaker, pointing out landmarks, telling funny stories and even having a sing song too. Edna didn't envisage this coach driver bursting into song. Maybe a different company was used because it was cheaper?

Joyce and her sister Margaret were sitting in their usual seats, right at the back with three of their other lively friends.

Edna looked across to the aisle and saw Milly and Doc Vic sitting happily together holding hands. She smiled and praised herself for contributing to their happiness. Her thoughts went back to their beautiful wedding reception last year. It was such a memorable day. A day that even Gerry couldn't ruin.

Twenty minutes into the journey, the coach turned onto the A47 and they were well on the way. The coach was noisy whilst the passengers chatted away until one gentleman indicated he needed the toilet. The coach driver was not amused because they were going to stop just after Peterborough for a comfort break. He ended up doing a premature stop at Morcott so the gentleman could get off to use the toilet. The gentleman then required his walker to assist him with the walk to the toilet, so the grumpy driver jumped off the coach and sorted out the walker from the luggage hold for him. Eventually, they were ready to set off again but when the driver went to turn the ignition key, nothing happened. He ended up having to call the office and arrange another coach to come and pick them all up. The irritable driver suggested all the passengers get off and go into the cafe as it was getting quite hot by then.

Finally, another coach turned up and luckily for the group, the driver that brought the replacement coach was to continue driving them. The grumpy driver had to wait with the broken down coach until assistance arrived. An hour after they had made the unplanned stop, they set off in the new coach with the new driver. By now it was ten o'clock so they were well behind schedule. The new driver used the microphone and introduced himself as Rick. He talked about the plan and times for the rest of the day. He was definitely more cheerful than the previous one. They still went ahead with the planned stop just past Peterborough, then arrived at the Sandringham estate around lunchtime.

As they were driving towards the grounds, there was a big notice which the driver stopped to read.

Gardens and grounds are closed for a week from July 5th whilst important maintenance is carried out. Sorry for any inconvenience caused.

Edna raised her eyebrows as she strained to read the notice. She wondered why a phone call to find out if everything was open had not been made. She knew that Anne would have made a call just to confirm before the day. The driver came over the loudspeaker again.

"Oh dear folks, I think I will have to take you all to the seaside for an ice cream!" he joked.

As he spoke the elderly gentleman again indicated he needed to use a toilet, which proved a problem with everywhere around being closed. Once the coach returned back on the main road to Hunstanton, the driver looked for a service area and then stopped. The gentleman required his walker again, getting out of the luggage hold. By the time he got back onto the coach, it was getting towards one o'clock. The coach carried on to Hunstanton, but with it being July and a beautiful day, the queue was quite long to get into the seaside resort.

Finally, the coach pulled up along the side of the road. The coach parks were full because coach places needed to be booked in advance. In this case the driver would have to go and park up somewhere away from Hunstanton and then return later to pick the group up. Edna looked at her watch when the coach stopped and it was just gone quarter past two. They had been on the coach for hours, just getting off to use the loo and have refreshments. She made up her mind she was not going on another trip unless it was organised by someone who could organise efficiently. Once the driver had switched off the engine, he made an announcement about times.

"Just to let you know that this coach has to be back at the depot for seven o'clock tonight because it was scheduled to be used for an evening trip and I have had a message to say that the coach which had broken down is now out of use. So I will be back to pick you up at ten to four. We must be left by four o'clock. I'm really sorry folks, it's out of my control."

Everyone groaned, and as quickly as they were able, made their way off the coach. By the time the driver had got the walkers and trolleys out of the luggage hold, it was half past two.

"Joan, we have an hour and twenty minutes, shall we just find a place to have a snack and look at the beach?" Edna said to her friend.

"There is little else we can do in the short time we have here," Joan replied.

They both walked with their shopping trolleys to a cafe which overlooked the sea. Once seated, they saw the sisters, Joyce and Margaret come in with their friends. They waved to Edna and Joan and sat down at an empty table nearby. Within ten minutes they were laughing loudly which was normal behaviour from the sisters and their friends. Their laughter was as usual infectious, making Edna and Joan smile. They all enjoyed their hour or so in the cafe, although it was a case of making the most of the short time they had not been on the coach. They all left together to walk back to the coach bumping into Vic and Milly as they neared the coach pick up spot. The coach was there and they all got back on. Once seated, the driver noticed there were two empty seats. By then it was nearing four o'clock so he was getting a bit anxious and enquired if anyone had seen the two ladies who were missing. Noone had, so the driver got off the coach and looked around. He noticed the two ladies rushing towards the coach, having lost their way. With everyone onboard, the coach set off at four o'clock as planned. Within twenty minutes the elderly gentleman wanted to use the loo again. The driver had no choice but to stop, which was an hour before the scheduled stop. Again, the gentleman was slow, so this held up the journey. The driver didn't hang around after that and they made a very quick comfort stop just before they reached Peterborough. Luckily for the driver, they reached the day centre by six thirty. Edna was back home at seven o'clock and immediately went straight to her comfortable armchair, exhausted, thinking what a disaster of a day. If Anne had organised it, it would have run so much more smoothly, she just knew it would have. The next thing she knew it was gone midnight when she woke up, still sitting in her chair in the dark.

The following Monday, after Edna had spent most of Sunday recovering from the stressful coach trip, she set off as usual on the short walk to the day centre. It was another lovely summer's day, the sky was a bright blue, with no clouds and there was little breeze. Despite the not so great day trip, she was ready to start a new week. She pushed her shopping trolley through the automatic doors as she entered the centre, and headed straight into the dining room, where she stopped dead in her tracks. She couldn't believe what she saw. It was the beautiful Diane, the previous centre Manager, talking to two other volunteers. When she saw Edna, she immediately left the others and rushed up to her and gave her a big hug and a kiss on the cheek.

"Oh darling Diane, I'm so pleased to see you, how long are you back home for?"

"I'm back for good Edna. My mother passed away six months ago, so I sorted out her affairs and have come home. But best of all the Trustees have offered me my old job back, they found out Gerry was doing things he shouldn't have and he has gone and I'm back! I'm just so glad to see you all again…it's been too long… and one of our first jobs will be to begin the meetings for another Christmas fashion show!"

Edna was incredibly happy as were all the other volunteers. 'Modelling at eighty' Edna thought to herself, 'mind you that's quite young compared with some of the others!'

"Bring it on Diane," she laughed, before heading to the store room to fetch out some table cloths. She looked at the piles of neatly ironed tablecloths and picked ones that they generally used for celebrations.

'It is a celebration' she thought. 'Our Diane is back…and Gerry has thankfully gone! What a fantastic start to a new week…'

Acknowledgements

—◊—

THANK YOU TO Joyce, Brian, Charlotte, Lenny, Val, Paul, Carol and Allyson for allowing me to put photos of themselves or their loved ones in this book.

Thank you Jo for helping me write Jospehine, Crazy Chauffeur. Even though we were apart, I had not laughed so much for a while writing this with your input… Girl Power!

Thank you to Bev and John for producing such a nutty daughter!

Thank you again to my friend, Suzanne Lambert and for her love of all animals.

Thank you Paul for the record shop memories.

Thank you to all my friends and relatives including those I keep in touch with on Facebook, here and in Australia for their support and kind comments about the stories I write to raise money and awareness for charities and disabilities.

A big thank you to the charity Colostomy Uk for their support.

As usual thank you Charlie, Steph and the staff at Jenno's, Blaby for the best coffee around and lastly thank you Bill and the girls for the Rosé evenings and The Rose Garden!

Live, Love, Laugh and stay positive!

Remembering inspirational people who have improved and saved the lives of others. Some mentioned in this book and also Dame Deborah James and Bill Turnbull RIP.

THE RED ROSE

A collection of short stories filled with the love, compassion, magical escapism and hope.

LINDA BOULTER

Proceeds from the sale of this book to the Joseph Cooper Trust

Proceeds to the Joseph Cooper Trust

Available from Troubador Publishing Ltd
Unit E2, Airfield Business Park
Harrison Road
Market Harborough
LE16 7UL

Telephone: 0116 2792299